2013

Miz Sparks Is
On Fire
and This Ain't
No Drill

Nancy Rawles

BLUE BEGONIA PRESS

Selah, Washington

llustrations by Sheila Arthur
Cover illustration by Michelle R. Brown
Cover design by Amy Peters
Book design and composition by
Integrated Composition Systems
Spokane, Washington

Library of Congress Cataloging-in-Publication Data

Rawles, Nancy, 1958-
Miz Sparks is on fire and this ain't no drill / by Nancy Rawles.
    p. cm.
ISBN 978-0-911287-68-4 (alk. paper)
1. Teachers--Fiction. 2. Public schools--Fiction. I. Title.
PS3568.A844M59 2012
813'.54--dc23

2012038531

Published in the United States
by Blue Begonia Press
in Selah, Washington
www.bluebegoniapress.com

for Ann Marie, my first teacher

"Every time you stop a school, you will have to build a jail. What you gain at one end you lose at the other. It's like feeding a dog on his own tail. It won't fatten the dog."—Mark Twain, 1900

Section One
Bum Rush

September

1 / Saved by the Bell

Did you hear what she said? Does she know where she's at? This is Muhammad Ali Elementary. We are fighters! If she thinks she's going to sashay in here with some more of that mumbo jumbo about measurable outcomes and high-stakes assessments, then she needs to reassess her assets. We're already up to our eyeballs in this hocus pocus. How many times can you measure children? When are you going to TEACH them? Please!

Queenie Johnson sat in the front row of parent chairs, texting Gloria Moore, who was sitting on the fourth row aisle. Gloria kept springing out of her seat to take video clips of Kiana, who was standing on the stage, directly to the right of the new principal, waiting to be introduced. Gloria's videos never turned out very well, but that didn't deter her. If Kiana was going to be a famous singer, like everyone reckoned she was, then Gloria needed to have footage from her early years. Besides, the parent chairs were uncomfortable. Since Gloria didn't answer her text right away, Queenie decided to send another one, this time to Sylvia Goodwin, who always had her phone at the ready. The good doctor was taking time away from orthodontia to attend the opening ceremonies, which were turning out to be a bust. Queenie peeped her in the second row, near the stairs, rolling her eyes. Now was the perfect time to strike. Dr. Goodwin tended to be impatient with everybody but her patients, so Queenie kept the message short.

> *How long do you think*
> *it'll take us to get rid of*
> *her?*

Sylvia's response was immediate.

> **February**

Queenie smiled broadly. A team of powerful Black women was all the world needed to right itself. Thank God the school had the benefit of their wisdom. She hit Sylvia again.

> *What kind of name is*
> *Camelione?*
> **Italian**
> *How do you know?*
> **Moonstruck**

Principal Camelione surveyed the people in the crowd. She could tell they weren't really with her. When she spoke about her plans for the school, eyes glazed over and heads drooped.

> *Cammareri*
> **Cappomaggi**

She had been with the District for only eight years, but she'd already climbed four levels of Dante's inferno and she could see the light at the end of the chimney.

> *Castorini*
> **Camelione**

The District had sent her to reverse "the culture of defeat" at Muhammad Ali.

Bring me the big knife.

For five years, the school had failed to meet the standards set by the federal No Child Left Behind Act. If test scores didn't rise as fast as the Mississippi in spring, the school would be added to the ever-burgeoning pile of failing American public schools.

**She's dying, but I can
still hear her big mouth.**

She felt like interrupting her own speech to strike the gong. Very few people seemed to notice the gong when she brought it in that morning and placed it on the stage. It wasn't a very big gong but it produced a powerful tone. She needed a way to get their attention.

*Leave the gun, take the
cannoli.*

If she didn't succeed, the District was prepared to close the school. If she succeeded, she'd been promised a promotion to the school of her dreams—two miles from her house, two assistant principals, an orchestra, tennis courts, its own radio station, a six-figure auction, and test scores that were the envy of NASA.

**My final offer is this:
nothing.**

If she failed, she would be demoted to vice principal of a remedial junior high school for students returning from juvenile detention.

*It's not personal, Sonny.
It's strictly business.*

With her left hand, she tugged on the back of her blouse. Sweat had caused the shimmering silk to stick to her. The air was oppressive. She felt certain someone had set her up.

Don Corleone
Vito Corleone

Michael Corleone
Connie
Fredo
Sing it, Little Whitney!

There was no mistaking Kiana's church-trained voice.

> *I believe the children are our future*
> *Teach them well and let them lead the way.*

The entire auditorium began to clap and sway. Gloria stood in the aisle filming. Whenever Kiana hit a false note, someone would encourage her upward and onward. *Sing it, girl. Don't hold back.* The unemployed fathers took every opportunity to shout their approval. They didn't like being dragged to school functions, so the singing was what they lived for. It meant the end was nigh. And for the women, it worked like a charm. It made the dads desperate to find work, any work, two or three shifts, as long as they wouldn't have to sit through this.

> *I decided long ago*
> *never to walk in*
> *anyone's shadow*
> *If I fail, if I succeed*
> *at least I live as I believe.*

Now the kids were on their feet. Fifth graders were pounding the floor with their thick-soled shoes. Kindergarteners were screaming their tiny little lungs out. Kiana threw back her shoulders and flung her arms wide.

> *No matter what they take from me,*
> *they can't take away my dignity.*

Mrs. Camelione shuddered at the enormity of the task before her. She was thirty-six and could forgive herself an occasional career miscalculation. It wouldn't happen again.

> *The Greatest Love of All*
> *is happening to me.*

*I found the greatest love of all
inside of me.*

Mrs. Camelione attempted to lead the wild clapping and undignified cheering, but she couldn't keep up with the syncopated beat. Meanwhile, Kiana redirected herself to announce the PTA's fall fund-raiser.

*The greatest love of all
is giving to your school
for only one dollar you can
buy five candy bars.*

Oh, dear. Veteran fifth-grade teacher Lavinia Sparks had her work cut out for her. Kiana, like the rest of her classmates, had spent her entire school career conceptualizing math instead of practicing it because that's what the experts at the University of Chicago said she should do. The message that math was a formal pursuit requiring a certain attention to facts had clearly not been conveyed. Kiana returned to her seat in the fifth-grade section, where she graciously received a host of high fives along with several enthusiastic slaps on the back.

"What's so special about her? Who told her she could sing?"

Antipathy Brown announced herself. Here she was, late on the first day of school, entering the auditorium with the ferocious growl and clumsy gait of a Tasmanian devil. Her nervous classmates pointed and giggled. Kiana ran to her mother.

Miz Sparks was going to have her hands full with this group. Good manners were always high on her list of imperatives, but this year they would have to be drilled. And from the size of these kids, she could see that self-discipline and restraint would be the only ways to keep them out of the hospital. She approached Antipathy from behind, turned her around, and before she could say anything else, enveloped her in a suffocating hug. She was not a particularly large breasted woman, but her mammaries were ample enough to do the trick.

"So lovely to see you, Antipathy." She pressed the girl's nose to her bosom.

Miz Sparks had seen Antipathy recently. They attended the same missionary Baptist church. In church, Antipathy sang louder than anyone else. She served as a greeter and acted in pageants. She would soon be old enough to join the adult choir. As soon as Miz Sparks released her, she gyrated down the aisle toward the stage.

"I can sing," she shouted. "Why don't y'all let me sing?"

Students squealed in delight as Miz Sparks followed in hot pursuit. But Antipathy was already climbing onto the stage. She introduced herself to the new principal. Mrs. Camelione recoiled as Antipathy stepped in front of her to take over the mic. The auditorium went silent. Everyone was waiting to see what the new principal would do.

"I don't believe you can sing," Mrs. Camelione remarked, as she tried to regain her composure. Antipathy's eyes narrowed.

"Go on, then, sing. What are you waiting for?" Mrs. Camelione waited with her arms crossed. She looked at her watch. Antipathy looked as if she might melt. She glanced at Miz Sparks, who was standing just below the stage. Her teacher nodded, and she began.

> *We are the champions, my friend*
> *And we'll keep on fightin' till the end*
> *We are the champions, We are the champions*
> *No time for losers 'cause we are the champions*

Her colleagues were dumbfounded. They had never seen a bully brought so low. If her voice hadn't been so shaky, so hopelessly off-key, they might have been able to redeem the song. As it was, they either looked on in horror or averted their eyes altogether. Antipathy didn't miss a beat.

"Did y'all even do the Morning Chant?" Her voice became deceptively soft and plaintive, but everyone knew what she was doing. In her humiliation, she had somehow found the strength to remain standing. The students leapt to their feet. They pumped their fists and shouted in unison, "Morning Chant, Morning Chant." Mrs. Camelione left the stage, hounded by a fearsome laughter that was usually reserved for playground battles. Antipathy called for quiet. "Let's begin," she said, swaying to her own inner pendulum. "Count off. One, two, three, and let's hear it for Muhammad Ali!"

We're the double greatest
What we're thinking is what we're becoming
Wake up, wake up, make your dreams come true
The will must be stronger than the skill
We have imagination, and our imaginations have wings
We can float like a butterfly and sting like a bee
I'm great, I'm bad, and I'm pretty
I'm the most superior, most scientific, most skillfullest
I'll stay in college, get the knowledge.
I'll stay there till I'm through.
If my mind can conceive it, and my heart can believe it,
Then I can achieve it.

The students waved their hands and cheered as their teachers urged them to sit down. Antipathy continued unabated. Now she was dancing across the stage like The Greatest himself.

"There's not a man alive who can whup me. I'm too fast. I'm too smart. I'm too pretty. I should be a postage stamp. That's the only way I'll ever get licked," she quoted her hero.

Before she could say another word, an enormous hand snatched the offender by the elbow and expelled her from the auditorium. Coach Birdsong was the de facto principal of the school and all the kids knew it. His presence was the only thing that stood between them and complete chaos. His efforts earned him a standing ovation.

Jake Minor, the vice principal, tried to refocus the audience by blowing a faint whistle. He was a one-time drum major, and this fact appeared to be his sole qualification for his current position. An elementary school resembled a marching band the same way scrambled eggs resemble an omelet. The basic ingredients might be the same—lots of noise, lots of bodies, a great deal of dissonance—but their arrangements were entirely different. Every time he tried to issue a command, he felt completely defeated. Formations never formed, the forward march was frequently confused with the backward march, and the parade never rested.

Mrs. Camelione had seen enough. She retook the stage, held her hand high to signal for quiet, and shouted into the microphone. "Everyone please sit down." The mic made that annoying sound it makes whenever it's irritated. Children covered their ears. Mrs. Camelione banged the gong as if she were banging a gavel. Parents bolted from their seats.

Queenie was outraged. She was old enough to remember a short-lived TV game show where the losing contestants were gonged.

> *No, she didn't!*
> **Uh oh false note**
> *Bring out the hook!*
> **How old do you think
> she is?**
> *35, 40, 45, old enough
> to know better . . .*
> **February can't arrive
> soon enough.**

Next, Queenie texted her husband, who had left the house at dawn to inspect the electrical work at a condominium remodel in another county.

> *You'll never believe
> what just happened . . .*

King Johnson glanced down at his phone before turning it off. He couldn't wait for Princess to graduate from fifth grade. Then, maybe, he could woo his wife back from the PTA, which was now her only love. King had other loves, but he didn't relish being unfaithful. He just couldn't compete with the intrigue of schoolhouse politics. He tilted his hardhat forward, made a note to cancel the unlimited texting plan, and turned his attention to a cross-wired circuit. He hated shoddy work. In order to avoid nuisance breaker tripping, he would have to un-nut the blacks in the junction box, separate them one at a time with his non-contact voltage tester, and re-establish the proper connections. The story of his life.

Coach Birdsong felt sorry for the new principal and even sorrier for himself. Why did the District harbor such contempt for its servants? Hadn't he been faithful? Hadn't he served twenty years without one stain on his record? One bad manager after another. He should have taken that offer from the Lynchburg Hillcats when he had the chance. Couldn't afford to. Had to take care of his dying mother. He was a stand-up guy with no desire so strong as his need to take care of women. Nurse Fine caught his eye and winked at him. Off to another rousing start. He put his fingers in his mouth and whistled. The auditorium immediately went quiet.

All eyes were on the Principal as she began to speak. This time, her tone was triumphant. "Students, faculty, staff, and parents of Muhammad Ali Elementary School, I am pleased to be your new principal. I look forward to interfacing with each and every one of you as we embark on an exciting new initiative of comprehensive overhaul."

The first graders fidgeted while the fifth graders nodded off. Miz Sparks sent Pedro to the office to ask Miss Juanita if she would kindly ring a bell.

Students at Muhammad Ali Elementary School were accustomed to waiting quietly for their teachers to dismiss them. If a teacher wasn't ready to dismiss them, there was nothing they could do about it. There were no clocks anywhere but the office. School was about learning, not about passing the time. Parents had to wait. Problems had to wait. Learning was taking place, and it was not to be interrupted by something as meaningless as a bell.

"If we actualize our academic standards by aligning our goals with District imperatives, we will upraise our learnings and incentivize our stakeholders to maximize our brand, thereby leveraging our product in the educational market placement of ideals."

The globular organs on Miz Sparks' face misted and fogged with aggregated condensation due to the astonishingly inept elocution.

In the waning days of summer, she had camped out in her classroom, ignoring the gossip from the other teachers. She had begged off the endless faculty meetings and staff development workshops, citing her recent widowhood as an excuse to bow out of impolitic society. Her plan had been to tolerate the new principal, no matter how absurdly incompetent she turned out to be. However when the bilingual aides simply shook their heads at the mention of Mrs. Camelione, she knew her toleration would be tested by the relentless hackneytudenization of language.

Miz Sparks loved language. Her entire curriculum was based on the learning of different languages. The language of math, the language of dance, the language of science, the language of art, the language of music, the language of place, the language of race, the language of space, the language of physics, the architecture of language, the language of grief.

"Let's medal in Olympic learnings!" Mrs. Camelione stood alone in her enthusiasm.

A bell sounded.

Suddenly, to the surprise of her students, Miz Sparks rose to leave. Though none of them could imagine doing anything so rude, they were grateful that their teacher wasn't bound by the same rules of decorum. They filed out silently. The entire school followed suit. As they exited the auditorium, Mrs. Camelione thanked them for giving her such a warm welcome.

Felicity Goodwin led Miz Sparks' class to the southeast portable, where they would be entombed for the rest of the year. Miz Sparks had taught Felicity's mother some thirty years before, and she was struck by the child's measured walk, head raised high on the slender neck, feet in perfect rhythm with the steadfast beat of her heart. In the child she could see the mother, her all-time best and most devoted student. Now, in her final year of teaching, she had been gifted with Sylvia's daughter.

As they passed the parking lot, Sylvia Goodwin waved and blew Miz Sparks a kiss. Miz Sparks reached up and caught it with her left hand, since her right hand was wrapped around the shoulder of Antipathy Brown, who didn't seem to want to go to class. Dr. Goodwin couldn't imagine where Miz Sparks found the strength, year after year, to deal with the fragile souls of her borderline-pubescent charges. It was easier to organize their teeth.

Long ago when she had attended the school, it was named Daniel Boone, and Miz Sparks was the young Miss Gaines. Fifth grade was the year Miss Gaines got married to a wise and dashing mailman. It was almost too much for Sylvia Cantwell, whose own parents were in the midst of a scalding divorce. If not for the love of Miz Sparks, Sylvia doubted she would have gone to college or married or had a child. She probably would have killed herself, as both her parents would later do.

By the time Tracy Goodwin arrived in her life, she was the face of thirty and the tired of seventy-five. His love had proved restorative. And Felicity was her joy.

Queenie was buzzing her phone again, but Sylvia was no longer interested in the new principal or in anything else about the school. Miz Sparks was the lone reason Felicity remained at Muhammad Ali Elementary School. No matter what happened this year, Dr. Sylvia Goodwin would grin her impossibly straight white teeth and bear it. She silenced her phone, but not before reading the final message.

> *Emergency PTA*
> *barbecue, my house,*
> *Saturday, 2-5pm,*
> *Board Members ONLY.*

2   /   Language Arts

Repeat after me: *Repeat after me*
Algonquin   *Algonquin*
Arapahoe   *Arapahoe*
Arawak   *Arawak*
Aztec   *Aztec*
Abijian   *Abijian*
Addis Ababa   *Addis Ababa*
Albuquerque   *Albuquerque*
Andalusia   *Andalusia*
Now, listen   *Now, lis'*
                                          Shhh, she said Listen

Thank you, Antipathy
S'il vous plaît, listen
Raise your hand when
you hear your name
Let me see who you are
Antipathy Brown
The first in town
Antipathy comes from
a Greek word meaning
"opposite feelings"
a contradiction, things
that don't go together
as in "oil and water"
or John the Baptist
and Herod's daughter   *That's from church, Miz Sparks*
That's right, my darling dear
And in this classroom, as far
as you're concerned,
every day is Sunday morn   *You want me to sing?*

When I give you the signal.   *When I give you the signal.*
Alps, Appalachians,
Atlas Mountains
Who's paying attention?   *Who's paying attention?*
Algernon Metoyer
Is Algernon here? Oh, dear,
I see you now, over there
I was looking for a boy
with a mustache, for
Algernon is a name from
French Normandy, meaning
"having a mustache" which
you don't have yet, however,
at the rate you're growing,
you may have one before
this year is over
Répétez, s'il vous plaît: *Répétez, s'il vous plaît*
Blackfoot   *Blackfoot*
Biloxi   *Biloxi*
Beijing   *Beijing*
Bahia   *Bahia*
Brisbane   *Brisbane*
Budapest   *Budapest*
Keep the beat going   *Keep the beat going*
Keep the boat rowing   *Keep the boat rowing*
Keep the flow flowing   *Keep the flow flowing*
We're swingin' with Basie   *Basie*
boppin' with Bird   *Bird*
blastin' the Beatles   *The Beatles*
breakin' to Beethoven   *Beethoven*
beltin' Broadway   *Broadway*
bravo for Barbra and   *Barbra*
somebody please bring   *Somebody*
Beyoncé some bling   *Beyoncé*
Bao Pham   *Bao Pham*
"treasure, precious"   *treasure, precious*

precious treasure
We're speaking
Chinese and
Vietnamese, too
because Bao means
"protection" and
I'm looking to you
to protect me, Bao
when I'm lost in
the Cascades or the
Canadian Rockies,
not to mention the
ones in Colorado,
when I'm high up in
the Caucuses looking
for Caucasians,
whatever the occasion
I'll stay clear with
Claire Davis-Walker
who's "clear and bright"
according to the French
I think they're probably
right, c'est possible, no?
Mais oui, ma cherie
Por favor repita
How come I only hear
Xochitl speaking
loud and clear?
And so can you
Por favor repita
Cordoba
Cuenca
Cuernavaca
You're going too fast.
You've got to work real
hard to keep up in my class

precious treasure
We're speaking
Chinese and
Shhh, it's not your turn

I don't think so, Miz Sparks

Over here, Miz Sparks

Mais oui.
Mais oui, ma cherie
Por favor repita

Xochitl speaks Spanish

¡Por favor repita!

Wait, Miz Sparks!

Coeur d'Alene
Cherokee
Choctaw
Cree
Cayuse
Cheyenne
Chippewa
Crow

Coeur d'Alene
Cherokee
Choctaw
Cree
Cayuse
Cheyenne
Chippewa
Crow
How come there's so many Cs?

Children, citizens,
countrywomen, compadres,
countrymen, compatriots,
colleagues, companions,
clowns, clods, and
counterfeiters,
don't you see?
The world is in love
with the letter C.
Now, repeat after me:
Cairo
Chiapas
Chiang Mai
Christchurch
Cincinnati
Conakry
Chicago
Cochabamba
Cucamonga
You're speaking Latin
You're speaking Malinke
You're speaking Ojibwe
You're speaking Quechua
You're speaking Tongva
Cynthina Gregory,
did you know Cynthina
is the name of the goddess

Cairo
Chiapas
Chiang Mai
Christchurch
Cincinnati
Conakry
Chicago
Cochabamba
Cucamonga
Latin
Malinke
Ojibwe
Quechua
Tongva
Cynthina
Be quiet.

of the moon? You have the
name given to Artemis, twin
sister of Apollo, born on
Mount Kynthos in the
Cyclades Islands
But where did they get
their beautiful names?

    It's just for Cynthina
    No, I don't. I'm named
    after my Grandma Cynthia
    and my Auntie Christina

    Beats me. But it sure wasn't
    from no Mt. Kynthos

Alas, you have a point,
But who are you really?
Fare attenzione
Bravo
Prego
De'André Jackson
from the Greek, Andreas
meaning "manly"

    That's Cynthina
    Fare attenzione
    Bravo
    Prego
    De'André Jackson
    from the Greek, Andreas
    meaning manly
    He ain't manly.

But he will be.
All of you will be.
Or womanly, perhaps.

    What you say?
    She called you a woman.
    You shut up, you mother.

Quincy Smith,
None of that in my class.
Neither one of you is a
woman or a mother and
most likely, you'll never become
either of those two most
wondrous beings, and yet
a manly man is better than
a donkey, so, that's enough
of your insolence, De'André.
No cursing or braying
in my class.

    She busted you, De'André.
    She called you an ass.
    At least, I ain't no donkey.

Efraím Rivera

Hebrew for "fruitful"
Elijah Ladu
Hebrew, meaning
"Yahweh is my God"
Elizabeth Yang
Hebrew, Elisheva,
"My God is abundance"   *That's from the Bible*
Thank you, Antipathy
In this class,
anaxnu medabrim ivrit   *Huh?*
Latine colloquamur   *Miz Sparks be talkin' crazy.*
when we say Felicity
Felicity Goodwin
"good fortune"
Is this the year of
good fortune?
Is it the year of the dog,   *It's the end of the world*
the horse, or the rabbit?   *It's the year of the dragon, Miz*
                                          Sparks
                                          It's the year of good fortune.

Bona fortuna   *Bona fortuna*
Carpe diem   *Carpe diem*
Cave canem   *Cave canem*
Cogito ergo sum   *Koji toe air go soon*
You're speaking Latin,
the language of the
Roman Empire,
a language only rarely
spoken nowadays but
you will know these terms
before this annus mirabilis
is finished.   *Miz Sparks, you makin' my*
                                          head hurt

Your head should be
hurting by the end of
each day, capiche?   *Capiche?*

If it's not hurting,
you're not working
hard enough, capiche?   *Capiche!*
In 1492, Columbus
sailed the ocean blue
Where'd he go to?   *Plymouth Rock*
Four score and seven   *Uhn uhn, he went to Boston*
years ago, would a rose   *No, he didn't, he went to*
                                         Columbus
by any other name smell   *I have an aunt in Columbus*
as sweet? Sweet as a   *Who cares?*
"white wave" named
Genevieve Dumlao,
a Celtic name, a woman
brave, "a woman of the
people" that's our
Genevieve. Wave to me,
sweetie. Are you new?   *Here I am, Teacher*
From where did you come?   *I come from the Philippines,*
                                         Ma'am

Complete sentences.
I like that. Make a note,
boys and girls. Genevieve,
we're very happy to
welcome you to our class.   *Welcome, Genevieve*
Wilkommen   *Wilkommen*
Bienvenue   *Bienvenue*
Welcome   *Welcome*
In Cabaret   *In Cabaret*
Au Cabaret   *Au Cabaret*
To Cabaret   *To Cabaret*
                                         Miz Sparks can sing!

Harry Wilson-Clarke
from Henry, Heinrich,
German for "ruler of home"
But I'm the only ruler here

Don't cry, Henry

Don't talk, De'André
How many languages do
we speak in this class?

So far, about forty

Thank you, Claire.
Isi Edwards
Isi is Choctaw,
meaning "deer."
You are as striking
as a deer, my dear.

Thank you, Miz Sparks

Jayan Patel,
Sanskrit for "victorious"

Patel is a famous name

Yes, sugar, but we're only
doing first names today.

Why?

Jerusalem Tadesse
Hebrew for "peace" also
the same in Amharic
Kenji Takahashi
Japanese for "study"
I know Kenji's going to
study hard in my class

Right!

Kiana Moore
Kiana, Hawaiian for Diana,
Roman goddess of the moon
Do we have two moon
goddesses in this class?
Leilani Lemalu, Hawaiian
meaning "heavenly flower"
I'm so glad to know a
heavenly flower like you.
I've taught all the Lemalus.

Yes, Miz Sparks

Marcus Thompson

Ooh, ooh, Miz Sparks

What is it, Marcus?

My name comes from Mars,
the Roman god of war

Very good, Marcus.

You come from Mars.

Don't be jealous, Renard.
We can't all come from Mars.
Marrakesh   *Marrakesh*
Missoula   *Missoula*
Mississippi   *Mississippi*
Molokai   *Molokai*
Netanya Miller-Resnick   *Netanya*
Hebrew, meaning
"gift of Yahweh"
Omar Martinez   *Omar*
from the Arabic name
Umar, meaning "life"
Pedro Brayboy   *Pedro*
from the Greek name
"Petros" meaning "stone"   *Pedro Gayboy*
Oh, Pedro, I imagine you're
tired of that tired joke?   *Yes, Miz Sparks. That's why*
                                    I don't like my name

Well, there's nothing wrong
with your name and nothing
wrong with you.
It's someone else's brain
and mouth that's all askew.   *I told you not to do that in Miz*
                                    Spark's class

Princess Johnson, a royal
name. Just remember, I'm
the only queen up in here.
                                    Ooh, she told you
                                    Shut up, Quincy. You are
                                    forbidden to speak to me.
                                    Ooh, Quincy, I guess she told
                                    you
                                    Shut up
                                    He likes her

That's enough, people.
I will have no romance in

my class. In fact, none of
you will participate in
romance until you are thirty
and have three degrees.
Are we clear?

Quincy Smith from Latin
"quintus" meaning "five"
I taught your daddy five
times five years ago. I'll
give you five . . . what?
Five cents. No, a penny
for your thoughts.

Renard Balthazar.
Renard is French for fox.
The bee will sting the fox,
if he bothers her too much.

Everything's reversible.
One thing leads to another.
Oh, brother, how many
dimensions are there?
Seven squared minus
four cubed equals . . . you're
kidding? A negative?
What gives? Math is poetry
I'll take times tables, angles,
anything but fractions.
Percentages, equivalents
Parentheses, exponents,
what comes next?
First, outer, inner, last,
I forget the rest.

*Ah, Miz Sparks, it ain't like
that*

500 dollars!

What's less than a penny?

*Whoa, she got you, Renard
At least, she didn't call me a
donkey*

Now, my head is spinning.

You look dizzy, Miz Sparks

We hold these truths to be
self-evident, that all men
are created equal. All men?
What about me?
My country 'tis of thee.
I know why the caged bird
sings. Life ain't been no
crystal stair. Do I care?
Goin' somewhere?
I declare,
Give me liberty or
give me death.
Liberté, egalité, fraternité,
Allons enfant de la patrie.
Angel Island Ellis Island
Alcatraz, All That Jazz
Give me your tired, your
poor, your huddled masses
longing to breathe free
I gotta be me.
I need a new pair of
glasses. Too bad how
sad your dad's been had.
The wind done gone and
I ain't yo' uncle.
Ain't I a woman?
Beautiful dreamer,
wake unto me.
What happens to
a dream deferred?
And what to the Negro
is your 4th of July?
I am nobody, who are you?
Are you nobody, too? I

am somebody. I am a man.   *You're not a man, Miz Sparks*
An astute observation.
We the People of the United
States. El pueblo unido,
jamás será vencido.
Go down, Moses, way
down to Egypt land.   *Miz Sparks is goin' crazy*
But how can you tell?
There are 192 nations in
the United Nations.
Memorize them. Soon there
will be 193. Learn to greet
each other in at least 12
different languages. Who
can name 100 indigenous
peoples of these lands?
The four great oceans and
the thirty-seven seas? The
seven great gulfs, the four
largest bays? The River
Nile and the Amazon, for
starters, the Yantze, the
Ganga, all sources of
water. Titicaca,   *Miz Sparks, you said a bad word*
Tanganyika, and
Gitchigumi, too.
Por favor repita comigo   *Por favor repita comigo*
so much depends upon   *so much depends upon*
a red wheel barrow   *a red wheel barrow*
glazed with rain water   *glazed with rain water*
beside the white chickens   *beside the white chickens*
William Carlos Williams   *William Carlos Williams*
so much depends upon
a red wheel barrow
glazed with rain water
beside the white chickens

so much depends upon
a red wheel barrow
glazed with rain water
beside the white chickens

And a road less traveled   *And a road less traveled*
And a bridge too far   *And a bridge too far*
God save the Queen
I have a dream
Does it dry up like a
raisin in the sun?
I will fight no more forever
Shall auld acquaintance be
forgot and never brought to mind?
Brother, can you spare a dime?
Sahara
Santiago
Repeat after me
Shanghai   *Shanghai*
I can't hear you
Serengeti   *Serengeti*
Say it like you mean it
Sicily   *Sicily*
That's sounding better
Sofia   *Sofia*
Tsibili   *Sibili*
Try it again
Ts, Ts, Tsibili   *Tsibili*
Thessaloniki   *Thessaloniki*
My sister-in-law is
from Thessaloniki   *Thessaloniki*
Saida Mohammed,
Arabic for "fortunate"
I feel fortunate to have
Saida in my class.
Serena Kruse,
from the Latin serenus,

meaning "tranquil"
Serena, thank you
for your patience.
Tuan Nguyen,
Vietnamese, meaning
"bright, intelligent"
Let's all endeavor to
live up to our names.
Will Robinson, Jr. has the
will, the desire given him
by his German name,
popular with the Vikings
who lived in France.
Have you heard of the
Vikings, my dear fellow?

> *Yes, Miz Sparks, who hasn't*
> *heard of the Vikings?*
> *Who are the Vikings?*

Xochitl Hernandez, Nahuatl
for "flower" and you are a
rare and interesting flower.

> *Muchas gracias, Profesora*

Zachary Jones, III
a Hebrew name meaning
"Yahweh remembers"
May Yahweh always
remember you, Zachary.

> *Thank you, Miz Sparks*

And last on my list . . .
Sometimes, last
Sometimes, first

> *The last shall be first*
> *And the first shall be last*

Very good, Antipathy.
Now, go sit down.
Zoe Allen, from the
Greek meaning "life"
a beautiful name, strong
like our Zoe. This is

your home, all of you.
Let no one defile it.
Zanzibar   *Zanzibar*
We played soccer on
the sands of Zanzibar.   *Zanzibar*
Isn't that the most beautiful
word you've ever heard?
Say it again.   *Zanzibar*

3 / First Order of Business

In Attendance:
Gloria Moore, President
Stephanie Anderson, Vice President
Dennis Takahashi, Co-Vice President
Queenie Johnson, Secretary
Tracy Goodwin, Treasurer
Sylvia Goodwin, Fundraising Chair
King Johnson, Chef Extraordinaire

Yours Truly: Welcome to the Seventh Annual Emergency Barbecue and September Meeting of the Officers of the Muhammad Ali Elementary School Parent Teacher Association. For those of you who've forgotten over the summer, I am Mrs. Purnella Johnson, Court Stenographer to the Stars, Queenie to you. So show me some deference.

This gathering would not be possible without the prowess of King Johnson on the grill. Thank you, Husband. Ribs and chicken for everybody but Mrs. Moore, who insists on having a veggie burger. We'll see how long that lasts. No Johnson Family Set-Your-Soul-on-Fire Kansas City Barbecue Sauce for Mrs. Anderson. Plenty of sauce for everybody else and double plenty on the vegetable burger. Hold the meat.

Thank you, Steph, for the mac and cheese. Always a joy. And Glo brought the green salad, if anybody feels like being healthy. Trace made his famous potato salad for those that aren't so inclined. And if you really want to do yourself some good, Syl's apricot pie is the jam.

Let us also recognize that we could not enjoy the sweet tastes of the Caribbean without the presence of one Dennis Takahashi, who was kind enough to bring his portable bar. Thank you, Taka. One mango margarita, no salt, if you please.

And, finally, Lord, let us give You all praise and solicitude for the blessings of Bethel Missionary Bible School, without whose services we would not be able to conduct this meeting in the absence of our children. Amen and Hallelujah. I would now like to turn these smoky proceedings over to Miz Veggie Burger She-self, Our Esteemed President, Gloria Moore.

Mrs. Gloria Moore: Thank you, Esteemed Secretary Queenie. In keeping with the spirit of this occasion, which you have so artfully declared, I'd like to employ Bobby's Rules of Order today, seeing how Robert couldn't make it. Do I have a motion?
   King Johnson: The chef so moves.
   Mrs. Gloria Moore: Do I have a second?
   Takahashi: Who's on first?
   Mrs. Gloria Moore: All in favor?
   Yours Truly: Aye, aye. The motion is carried. It's time to eat, y'all.

Pause.

Note: The meeting was suspended while everyone dished their plates. I am not taking proper minutes because I want to eat and drink like everybody else, and this is an emergency meeting wherefore people should be free to express their opinions without having to enter it into any official record. Once everybody has their food and drinks, we'll begin our informal conversation about the goings-on at MAES. In the meantime, Gloria had a banana daiquiri. Stephanie only drank water, not even a lemon in it. Sylvia had a Cuban drink. Tracy had a Long Island Iced Tea. I never took him for a drinking man. King had the usual. Taka drank beer.

Resume.

Glo: So why are we here, you ask? Because our way of life is under threat. I'm not saying all the rumors are true. Some rumors are false. But like stereotypes, rumors exist because people strive to live up to them. A reliable District source has informed me that our new principal has a whole file cabinet dedicated to all the complaints against her. And she's about to need another one.
   Syl: That sounds like an exaggeration.
   Glo: And in addition to that, I hear she eats small children for breakfast.

Syl: Where do you get such foolishness?

Glo: From Miss Juanita in the office. She said Camelione comes in mad, like she's been eating small children for breakfast.

Syl: Next.

Glo: But I'm not through.

Syl: You wasted your turn. Next.

Steph: I hear her blond comes out of a bottle.

Syl: Next.

Trace: You mean to tell me, y'all called an emergency meeting to gossip?

King: You got something against barbecue?

Yours: Just hold on, Goodwin. You know us better than that. It's gonna get better. Come on, y'all, give me something I can work with.

Steph: Okay, for real, I hear she forced the teachers at Rachel Carson to stop teaching *Silent Spring.* And they were only reading the first three pages, you know, "A Fable for Tomorrow." "A grim specter has crept upon us almost unnoticed . . ."

Glo: That's creepy. That might scare the children.

Steph: Do you even know what her book is about?

Glo: You don't have to get testy with me. Of course, I know what *Silent Spring* is about. It's a science book, and that's why I've never read it. Just because you're a scientist and you like dressing up in those little white coats . . .

Steph: I'm not a scientist. I just like to read.

Syl: People, people, let's get back on point.

Trace: Yes, what Stephanie said is important. I'd like to second it. If people start censoring what books our children can be exposed to, I mean, what good can come of that?

Syl: But how do you know it's true? How do you know she censored *Silent Spring?*

Steph: Because that's not all. She tried to take away Mildred Taylor.

Glo: Oh, no. Is she out of her mind? Tell me she is not trying to take away *Roll of Thunder, Hear My Cry.* I'm sorry, but Mildred Taylor is here to stay. I will defend that book with my dying breath. What does she want to replace it with? Little Black Sambo?

King: She needs to take her hands off the books.

Yours: That's right. Here's to the chef.

All: To the chef.

King: Does anybody want some more ribs? I didn't buy all this meat for y'all to let it sit around in the pan looking lonely.

Trace: I'll take some more, brother. I can't get enough of that sauce.

King: Now you're talking. What about you, little man?

Taka: I'm cool, man. I'm cool.

Syl: Whose turn is it?

Glo: Isn't anybody going to offer me some more?

King: What you want, baby doll?

Glo: I'll take some more of that macaroni and cheese.

Steph: Isn't it good? It came out good this time.

Glo: Uh huh. But the one you made last Christmas was even better.

Steph: That was the Christmas before last. I didn't make any last Christmas. I was in the hospital having a cyst removed from my ovary.

King: Do we have to share?

Glo: Was that just last Christmas? My, how time flies.

Syl: Don't it, though? Can we get on with it?

Steph: I hear she wants to cancel Christmas.

King: Who wants to cancel Christmas?

Steph: The principal. She already canceled Halloween, now she's trying to cancel Christmas.

King: Why is she trying to cancel Christmas?

Steph: Because some of the kids aren't Christian.

Glo: I beg your pardon. Is there any evidence that the non-Christians object to Christmas?

Syl: Well, as one of two non-Christians in attendance, I can assure you, while Christmas is not celebrated in our house—we celebrate Kwanzaa, but that's beside the point—we don't object to Christmas, but I can see why some people might.

Yours: What people? The Mexicans are Christian. The Samoans are Christian. The Filipinos are Christian. The Ethiopians are Christians. Who is she talking about? The lesbian Jews? All the gay people I know love Christmas. They go straight from Christmas to Mardi Gras. The Chinese don't care. They let everybody celebrate Chinese New Year.

Why can't everybody celebrate Christmas? I don't see the problem.

Taka: We celebrate everything in our house.

Yours: That's because y'all is mixed up.

King: Come on, baby. Don't do the brother like that. Taka, I think you gave her too much salt.

Syl: The times, they are a wastin'.

Trace: She means the Muslims. Muslims don't celebrate Christmas.

Glo: How does she know what they do in the privacy of their own homes?

Trace. We should have a Muslim on the Board. It would silence our critics.

Yours: What critics?

Trace: You know, the people who say we're a members-only club, if you know what I mean.

Yours: No, I don't know what you mean.

Glo: He's talking about the White Folks, Queenie. You know, "diversity."

Yours: Lord, today. This is the price we pay for integration. But how is getting a Muslim on the Board going to diversify us when our Muslims are Black. We'll still be an All-Black Board.

Taka: Excuse me. I beg to differ.

Yours: What you want, Dennis?

Taka: I'd like to challenge the preceding comment. We're not ALL black.

Glo: What's he talking about?

Yours: Knock it off, Takahashi, you know you Black. You got mixed kids, you a jazz musician, and you walk like a brother. You know you be a brother man. Stop trying to confuse the issue. Now what were we talking about?

Syl: We were talking about getting a Muslim on the Board.

Steph: How about that lady who's always at school?

Syl: What lady?

Steph: I don't know her name, but she always looks so pretty, the way she dresses.

Glo: You'd think a scientist could be more precise.

Steph: I keep telling you I'm a pharmacist, not a scientist.

Glo: Chemicals, white coats, same difference.

Steph: You know who I'm talking about. The one with all the kids. Sister can put together anything, and it still looks good.

Yours: You mean Mohammed. She must have come here thinking it was a Muslim school.

Steph: I really don't know how she does it. Checks with plaids with flowers with polka dots. And those designer silk scarves. If I went out like that, I'd looked like a crazy person.

Yours: But she looks good, don't she? You would look like a fashionista terrorista.

Syl: Can we please get past the stereotypes?

Yours: I beg your pardon. Weren't you the one texting me about Mafioso?

Syl: I was bored.

Yours: Well, you can be bored again. Because I have something I need to say. There are entire ethnic groups that shouldn't wear certain clothes. There. I've said it.

Taka: Isn't Mohammed a man's name?

Yours: Her last name is Mohammed, dummy. She's from Somalia. All Somalis are named Mohammed.

Syl: That's not true. I know a Somali named Ali.

Trace: That's Abdi, not Ali.

Syl: No, I'm not talking about Abdi. I'm talking about Ali.

King: Okay, you two, let's settle down. No marital disputes at the dinner table. Anybody want some more chicken?

Taka: How 'bout another drink?

Yours: I once knew a fellow named Mohammed Mohammed. I think I'd like to try one of those how-do-you-call-'em, that Cuban thing.

Taka: A cigar?

Syl: I think she means a mojito.

Steph: I knew an Israeli named Shalom Shalom. May I have more water, please?

King: Remember Boutros Boutrous Gali?

Glo: This veggie burger is lousy. King, you better lay some chicken on me. 'Cause you do not know how to cook a veggie burger.

King: You're the one who ordered it well done.

Syl: We need to get back on task. Who's going to ask Mrs. Mohammed to join the Board?

Taka: I can ask, but I think a woman should probably do it. And if I may point out, the Board could use a few more men.

Yours: Takahashi, what are you going on about? We got two men. How many do we need? Besides, what man has the kind of time you have? I mean, when do you start work? 10 pm? And when do you get off? Four hours later? Who else has hours like those?

Glo: Why don't we ask King to join the Board?

King: That's very kind of you, Glo, but I'm afraid I have other obligations.

Glo: What other obligations?

King: That's for me to know and you to find out.

Yours: Gloria Moore, you stop flirting with my husband this minute, do you hear me? He's much too pretty to be on this Board.

Taka: Hey, wait a minute. I think I should be insulted by that.

Glo: What about Goodwin? He's pretty.

Yours: He needs to cut those dreads. If you cut those dreadlocks, Tracy, you might be a good-lookin' fellow up under there.

Syl: No comment.

Trace: Speaking of men on the Board, I really do need to think about quitting. I don't have any time on my hands.

Glo: He's got lotion on his hands. Look, how soft his hands are. I wish I had . . .

Trace: These hands are very busy, unfortunately, with all kinds of suffering.

Glo: Sylvia, I don't know how you can let your husband be a physical therapist. Don't you worry about the women?

Syl: Only you, Gloria. Only you.

Trace: I know plenty of men who've got plenty of excess time on their hands, but they're not the kind you'd want on your Board.

Yours: Oh, here we go again. You need to stop talking bad about Brown. Why does Brown have to be part of every meeting. Can't you give the brother a break?

Trace: We went to school together, that's all. He's been drinking since he was eleven.

Taka: Now, that ain't right. Who wants another round?

King: At least, he doesn't drive. I'll take another.

Trace: He can't drive. He don't have no license, no insurance, and he smashed up all his cars.

Syl: Lord, chile. My people, my people. Can we please get back to business?

Steph: I hear she wants to eliminate the Morning Chant.

Syl: Why would she want to do that?

Steph: She says it's not grammatically correct.

Yours: What does that have to do with anything?

Syl: I remember when we instituted the Morning Chant. In fact, my class had a hand in writing it.

Taka: Maybe, we could change a sentence or two.

Yours: Why? It's a positive chant. We're not talking about white devils.

Taka: Yeah, but that last line—that was Jesse Jackson.

Glo: You're kiddin'.

Taka: No, Madam President, I assure you I'm for real. "If my mind can conceive it, if my heart can believe it, I know I can achieve it because . . .

All: I am somebody!

Glo: Ain't that nothin'? Takahashi has to come up here and tell us our history.

Trace: Thank you, my brother. Put it here.

Taka: No problem, my homie. Any time.

Glo: Well, I'm glad we got that straight.

Syl: Should we change it?

Yours: No way. The kids don't know any better.

Glo: And I can personally testify that Jesse wouldn't mind.

King: You telling me you and Jesse are tight?

Glo: Walked right up to him at Midway Airport and shook his hand. Now in his day, he was one beautiful man. His photos do not do him justice.

Taka: Jesse flew out of Midway? That must have been a long time ago.

Syl: Is there another item of business? Besides Jesse?

Steph: Just one more thing. I hear she wants to change the name of the school.

Glo: Whuuuuut?

Steph: You heard me. Rumor has it she wants to change the name of the school. She says it's not appropriate for children.

Yours: Is she crazy? Our ancestors fought for that name.

Syl: Our predecessors.

Yours: You know what I mean. Why do you always have to act so superior?

Glo: King, when you gonna give me the recipe for your sauce?

Yours: (from Memory) Shut up, Gloria. This is serious business. You need to act presidential. We cannot let her change the name of our school. It's our school. Can't they let us have anything? What do they even want with our school? Why are they trying to shut us down? I mean, sometimes, I can't take it. I really can't.

Glo: Damn, Queenie, she ain't gonna get away with it. What she want to change it to?

Steph: Carter Woodson.

Glo: Ain't gonna fly. I mean, I love me some Carter Woodson, but he ain't no Ali.

Syl: This is ridiculous. What's wrong with Ali? Malcolm X has schools named after him.

Taka: Elementary schools?

Syl: Yep. One in D.C. and one in Berkeley.

King: They got schools named after Malcolm X? What's their motto? "By any means necessary?"

Syl: That's right. Education, by any means necessary. Now, that's a radical idea. No joke.

Yours: Why does she think she can get away with this? Bill Clinton has several elementary schools named after him. Is he appropriate for children?

Glo: But he was the President.

Yours: Muhammad Ali could have been President. The country just wasn't ready for him. The wars would have ended sooner, I can tell you that. Isn't that what he said? They called him a Communist.

Syl: Hell, they called Dr. King a Communist. They called Eleanor Roosevelt a Communist. They call Barack Obama a Communist.

Trace: A Socialist. They call Barack a Socialist.

Glo: What's the difference?

Trace: I'm a Socialist. Norwegians are Socialists. Jesus was a Socialist.

Glo: You're kidding? How 'bout that!

Syl: Communist, Socialist, whatever and whatnot, that's just a code word for we-don't-want-him. I mean, this isn't Mike Tyson. This is Muhammad Ali, for crying out loud. The brother is smart. He's a beautiful, self-educated, self-actualized person.

Trace: Do you think it's the Muslim thing?

Syl: I never thought of that.

Trace: Maybe, it's the Muslim thing.

Syl: I think you may be on to something.

King: But what about Malcolm? Wasn't he a Muslim?

Trace: But he didn't change his name.

King: Yes, he did. He changed it to X.

Trace: But that's not an Arabic name.

King: Do you think it's an Arabic thing?

Glo: Maybe, it's an Arabic thing.

Yours: Why can't you name a school after an Arab? Wasn't Omar Khayyám an Arab? Bet you didn't think I knew him, did you? Arabian Nights, Aladdin . . .that used to be popular in my day.

Syl: Omar Khayyám was Persian. He wrote the Rubaiyat. Nobody knows who wrote Arabian Nights. I think it's Persian as well.

Yours: You are missing my point intentionally.

King: Lord, Lord, here they go . . .

Syl: Do you mean intentionally or entirely?

Yours: Both. Didn't Einstein invent the nuclear bomb? How many schools they got named after Einstein? Nobody's complaining about him.

Syl: Einstein didn't invent the nuclear bomb. They just used some of his formulas to invent it. It was unintentional.

Trace: Give it a rest, Syl.

Yours: Unintentional? How can you invent a nuclear bomb unintentionally? That thing was planned.

Steph: She's got a point. I don't think we can argue with that.

Glo: I second the motion.

Yours: You're not supposed to second anything. You're the Board President.

Glo: Where does it say the Board President can't second whatever she wants to second?

Yours: There wasn't even a motion on the table.

King: Calm down, darlin'.

Yours: I am calm. I'm not listening to a word any of you say. But it just so happens I need to take a little break, anyway. Y'all be quiet while I'm gone. No tellin' tales behind my back.

King: You mean, behind your tail.

Yours: I heard that, King Johnson.

Glo: Girl, go on and do your business before I have to set you straight.

Taka: Anybody for another drink?

Pause.

King: I bet Joe Louis has a school named after him. The Brown Bomber Academy.

Taka: I don't know about a school, but I bet he has a bomb named after him.

Yours: I heard that, you two.

King: Come on, little man. At least, wait till she's out of earshot.

Resume.

Yours: Okay, I've thought things over in a very calm frame of mind, and I'm sorry, but Camelione needs to go. That's my final decision. Who's with me? We need to plan a strategy. How long did it take us to get rid of that last one?

Steph: It doesn't matter. They'll just send us another one. Don't you know they're trying to kill the school? That's why they brought in that new superintendent . . . so he could kill some schools.

Taka: Can I get you something else to drink, Queenie? You barely touched your mojito.

Yours: Thank you, Dennis. I'd like to try some of what Tracy's having, some of that iced tea. It looks awfully good.

Glo: I move that we meet with the principal at our earliest convenience and let her know the importance of keeping the school's traditions, including the name.

King: I second the motion.

Glo: All in favor?

Yours: We haven't had a discussion.

King: What's there to discuss?

Yours: I have an amendment. This is not just about traditions, this is about children and how they learn. You're forgetting that we grew up in a time when Black Pride was all the rage. Black was Beautiful. Now, we've got a Beautiful Black President with a Beautiful Black First Lady and Two Beautiful Black First Children with their Beautiful Black First Grandmother, all living up in the Beautiful Big White House. Some folks think we have arrived. But look at our schools. People, look at our schools! They're trying to take away Mildred Taylor. Doesn't that just make you a little bit scared? They're trying to defeat Muhammad Ali. Doesn't that make you a tiny bit angry? Our kids don't know how to fight anymore. Don't you remember when we were coming up? Everyday, the old folks would tell us, "Go kick their asses. Make 'em pay." It wasn't good enough to play. We had to win. But now they've rigged the game so we can never win. NO CHILD LEFT BEHIND. Don't you get it, people? Unscramble the letters, and it all comes through, clear as a bell: I BEHOLD A THIEF IN DC. They're trying to bring down the Black Man. It's a conspiracy. Stolen elections, corporate crime, bogus foreclosures, widespread fraud, mass unemployment . . . the Race War has begun!

Pause. Resume.

Trace: Okay, this is getting way out of hand. I think it's time for us to go. Syl?

Syl: You left out an N and added an A.

Yours: What did she say?

Syl: You left out an N and added an A. I think it spells: DEBT HI ON FED INC HILL

Trace: Leave it, Syl.

Syl: I think I've got an extra I.

Steph: I hear she's planning to take away recess.

King: Come on, Queenie. It's time for our nap.

Glo: The girl has a point.

Trace: We'll see y'all next time.

Taka: I'm feeling like another drink. Would anyone else like another drink?

4 / Camelione v. Sparks: *Round One*

From: "Camelione, Diana" <camelioned@districtschools.org>
To: "Sparks, Lavinia" <sparksl@districtschools.org>
Subject: Discipline
Date: September 26 8:27 AM

Dear Mrs. Sparks,

This morning, I encountered a student of yours attempting to leave the cafeteria before finishing her cereal. When I asked her to return to her table, she refused. When I warned her she would be subject to lunch detention if she didn't obey my order, she laughed and said, "You can't make me." When I asked her name, she refused to say.

At this point, I summoned Major Minor via walkie-talkie. He met the student as she bolted for the 5th grade portables. When he attempted to block her path for the purpose of questioning her, she threw the cereal at him and tried to run him down. My admonitions to cease and desist were met with a string of expletives followed by a series of threats. Fortunately, one of our special ed teachers who heard the commotion was able to successfully restrain the girl, who was later identify as the same Antipathy Brown who earlier this month was given in-house suspension for disrupting the assembly.

A quick review of her files indicated that Miss Brown has met with censure before and that she has continually flouted the rules of this District. I have no choice but to suspend her for three days. Please send her books and assignments to the office so that I can give them to her parents when they come to remove her.

In addition, I would like you to place on my desk tomorrow morning a disciplinary plan for this student and any other similarly disruptive students you may have in your class. If you are unable or unwilling to implement an effective program of discipline for each of your students, I'm sure we can come up with a plan of assistance. I have asked Major

Minor to check in with your class from time to time so the students will grow accustomed to a more focused environment. It is only by working together that we can guarantee that our students have the skills and habits needed to succeed.

Sincerely,
Diana Camelione, Principal

From: "Sparks, Lavinia" <sparksl@districtschools.org>
To: "Camelione, Diana" <camelioned@districtschools.org>
Subject: Re: Discipline
Date: September 26 8:43 AM

Dear Mrs. Camelione,

Forgive me for not sending you the following memo regarding Miss Brown.

> She doesn't get enough to eat.
> She walks to school because she lives too close (within two miles) for the transportation office to assign a school bus to pick her up. The family can't afford the city bus fare.
> She was recently reunited with her parents after spending six months in foster care.
> The family lives in the basement of a house owned by a distant cousin who rents it out to dubious characters that come and go all hours of the day and night.
> The basement has no heat.
> The yard is home to a pit bull that is perpetually tied to a long rope.
> She doesn't get enough sleep.
> Her parents seldom work.
> Mom is in desperate need of dental care.
> Dad is in desperate need of rehab.
> Her parents both furtively love and desperately need her.
> She's the only one in her family who can read and write.

I'm afraid I can't abide your decision to suspend Miss Brown for three days. It is my opinion that Miss Brown, perhaps more than any of my other students, needs to be in school every day. This is where she gets her meals and her exercise. This is where people laugh at her jokes. This is where her every need is attended to, not always well, but always in time. For these reasons and many more, I am requesting you reconsider your decision to suspend Antipathy Brown.

Respectfully,
Lavinia Sparks, 5th Grade Teacher

From: "Camelione, Diana" <camelioned@districtschools.org>
To: "Sparks, Lavinia" <sparksl@districtschools.org>
Subject: Re: Discipline
Date: September 26 9:10 AM

Dear Mrs. Sparks,

I am well aware that too many of our students do not live in ideal situations and are not adequately resourced. If they are going to leave behind their poor station, they will have to adopt middle-class values, for example the practice of being on time and the habit of respecting authority. I have the data to prove this.

If Miss Brown has to eat her breakfast at school, she will need to leave her home earlier in order to get to class on time. No exceptions. Food must be eaten in the cafeteria, not in the classroom. No exceptions. I was willing to forgive Miss Brown her first infraction and let her go with a warning, but when she threatened an adult, I had to draw the line. Please do not try to second guess my decision to suspend her. The sooner she gets the message that her behavior will no longer be tolerated, the better we can expect her to conform to the rules.

Speaking of rules, it has come to my attention that your students were seen running around the playground yesterday afternoon with no teacher in sight. May I remind you that children are to be supervised at all times. In addition, only students in grades K, 1, and 2 are entitled to an afternoon recess. Students in grades 3, 4, and 5 are allowed one 10-minute recess every morning. Their additional exercise minutes are fulfilled by forty minutes a week for PE and their daily 15-minute lunch recess. This accumulates to 2 hours and 15 minutes per week of exercise or an average of 27 minutes a day, 2 minutes more than the District requires.

Diana Camelione, PhD and Principal

"To penetrate and dissipate these clouds of darkness,
the general mind must be strengthened by education."
                                              Thomas Jefferson

From: "Sparks, Lavinia" <sparksl@districtschools.org>
To: "Camelione, Diana" <camelioned@districtschools.org>
Subject: Re: Discipline
Date: September 26 11:16 AM

Dear Mrs. Camelione,

With all due respect, perhaps I am the person who should be suspended. It is I who told Antipathy to come to class on time, even if she hadn't finished her breakfast.

Regarding the new rule prohibiting eating in the classroom, I'm wondering what we're to do about birthdays, snacks, and rainy-day recess. Has a policy been instituted regarding PTA-sponsored pizza parties for classes that raise the most funds during the annual cookie dough drive or PTA-sponsored "fuel" during the fall and spring testing periods, or PTA-sponsored bake sales during the quarterly book sales in the library? Please advise.

Speaking of the library, has it been exempted from the new policy regarding consumption of food and beverages? I'm concerned about the presence of food at the faculty meetings, which routinely take place in the library. I feel it is my duty to inform you that for a number of years in the not-so-distant past, that portion of the main building had a significant problem with pest control. It's too bad we don't live in one of those countries where children go home for lunch. That would solve so many problems.

In reference to the rumors about my students running around the playground unsupervised, I was the one who sent them running. It was apparent to me that they needed to move. I arranged for two very responsible students to lead the line of eight in a short run around the playground before returning to their water bottles. As far as I can tell, they conducted themselves beautifully. I received compliments from several teachers who saw them run past their classroom windows. Did you receive a complaint about their behavior? Please let me know if this is the case. I would be happy to address the complainant directly.

Lastly, I would be remiss if I didn't urge you to avoid the perception of unjust treatment. It has been pointed out to me by several parents that acts judged worthy of suspension when performed by African American students barely cause a blink of the eye when performed by European and Asian American students. Indeed, I have witnessed the same myself—students referred to the nurse to rest and recoup following breakdowns, meltdowns, screaming fits that landed them in your office, while others were swiftly shown the door following similar collapses. Is it the cursing you find egregious or the unnerving lack of repentance? Believe me, there is not a person on this staff who is not offended by these postures, whether presented by African American children or by any others. This is my point. Both children and adults perceive fairness not only in reference to the way they are treated but also in light of the contrasting treatment of others who appear to be more favored.

Personally, hurling chairs is where I draw the line. How is it that chair-throwers walk away with a warning while tongue-waggers get the boot?

Sincerely,
Lavinia Sparks, M.Ed.

"Cauliflower is nothing but cabbage with a college education."
Mark Twain

From: "Camelione, Diana" <camelioned@districtschools.org>
To: "Sparks, Lavinia" <sparksl@districtschools.org>
Subject: Re: Discipline
Date: September 26 12:54 PM

Mrs. Sparks,

Please do not change the subject. I resent the insinuation that I am at fault for singling out African American students when it comes to discipline. I have never in my life been a racist.

Regarding the serious matter of your students running wild, I refer you to the *District Handbook for All School Personnel,* Chapter 7, Paragraph 13:

"Children shall be supervised at all times. District personnel are legally responsible for all children while they are in school or engaged in a school-sponsored activity, for example, on a field trip, at camp, or while riding a school bus to and/or from school. District personnel include teachers, substitutes, staff members, instructional assistants, school bus drivers, playground supervisors, counselors, coaches, school nurses, social workers, lunch room attendants, security guards, and administrators. District personnel do not include parents, friends, visitors, itinerant artists, or any members of the public who are not properly credentialed."

I am re-attaching the memo I sent to all teachers and staff members last week regarding food in the classroom. If you have any further questions, please do (not) hesitate to contact me.

Dr. Diana Camelione, Your Principal

MEMO TO ALL TEACHERS AND STAFF
REGARDING FOOD IN THE CLASROOM

There will be no food allowed in the classroom for the following reasons:

1. The janitor can clean each classroom only every other day.
2. Some children have food allergies.
3. There is an obesity epidemic in our country.
4. Sugary snacks and juices are the cause of this epidemic.
5. In the past, our building has had a problem with rodents and sugar ants.

Furthermore, to guarantee the cleanliness of our classrooms and the health of our students:

Birthdays will no longer be celebrated in class but may still be celebrated at lunch recess. Parents are welcome to bring healthy snacks for every student in the class. Healthy snacks are limited to fruit (no fruit cups), vegetables (no dip), and crackers (light salt). No balloons are allowed.

From: "Sparks, Lavinia" <sparksl@districtschools.org>
To: "Camelione, Diana" <camelioned@districtschools.org>
Subject: Re: Discipline
Date: September 26 3:41 PM

Dear Mrs. Camelione,

I find admirable your desire to encourage our students to alter their eating habits in favor of more healthy and nutritious food. I support these efforts. I also have a few suggestions on how to improve our students' overall well-being:

1. Healthy and nutritious kid-friendly food in the cafeteria. Milk without bovine growth hormones.

2. The restoration of the garden program and the rehiring of our part-time garden educator, who did a remarkable job of explaining nutrition, showing students how to grow organic kitchen gardens, and inviting them to feast on salad greens any time they visited the school garden. This was an award-winning program, partially funded by private donations. I must confess that I don't understand your decision to do away with it.

3. A snack allowance that would allow teachers to purchase nourishing snacks to pass out at recess. In my experience, many of our students lack the protein they need to make it through the school day. The cinnamon rolls, cereals, and breakfast bars offered in the cafeteria before school are full of sugar and notably lacking in nutrition. I suggest teachers be provided with pocket money to purchase fruit and cheese for students to eat during the morning recess. This would go a long way toward staving off the hunger and malnutrition that distract children from their studies. Perhaps the PTA would be willing to partially fund this expenditure. I would be willing to give up the expensive new math curriculum in favor of a finer dining experience.

4. A change in the quarterly fund-raiser from cookie dough to oranges or wrapping paper.

5. Water coolers in every classroom. Often when students feel hun-

Bum Rush / 49

gry, they are actually dehydrated. As you know, the school has old pipes, and only a few of the water fountains actually work. It is my understanding that you were able to get the District to provide water coolers for the classes at Rachel Carson after parents hired an independent scientist to test for lead and mercury in the water. Might you be able to convince the District to do the same for Muhammad Ali? Our semiannual complaints have gone nowhere. Would you recommend we also hire a scientist to test our water?

Regards, LS, M Ed

From: "Camelione, Diana" <camelioned@districtschools.org>
To: "Sparks, Lavinia" <sparksl@districtschools.org>
Subject: Re: Discipline
Date: September 26 4:27 PM

LS— This discussion has veered far away from the original topic of your student's suspension. If you have additional concerns, please bring them to the attention of Vice Principal Minor. He can put them on the agenda for the next faculty meeting.

  Until then, please prioritize all emails and memos coming from this office. The students can hardly be expected to follow the rules when teachers are out of compliance. —DC

From: "Sparks, Lavinia" <sparksl@districtschools.org>
To: "Camelione, Diana" <camelioned@districtschools.org>
Subject: Re: Discipline
Date: September 26 4:33 PM

D—I'm grateful for the chance to discuss issues of vital concern to our school. I'm sure you will agree with me that our goal is to provide a safe, healthy, and welcoming environment for all of our families and to empower our children through learning. Therefore, please be so kind as to give my student, Antipathy Brown, another opportunity to comply with the newly minted rules, with which she may not yet be fully familiar, as is true for me as well. —L

From: "Camelione, Diana" <camelioned@districtschools.org>
To: "Sparks, Lavinia" <sparksl@districtschools.org>
Subject: Re: Discipline
Date: September 26 4:44 PM

If I have not made myself clear: foul language will not be tolerated. Rude behavior has no place in an institution of learning. You do your student no favors by feeling sorry for her and permitting her to behave badly. I grew up in circumstances not unlike Miss Brown's. If my teachers had pitied me, I would have never realized my potential.

Diana Camelione, PhD

"Self-pity is our worst enemy and if we yield to it,
we can never do anything wise in this world."
Helen Keller

From: "Sparks, Lavinia" <sparksl@districtschools.org>
To: "Camelione, Diana" <camelioned@districtschools.org>
Subject: Re: Discipline
Date: September 26 5:05 PM

Dear Principal Camelione,

You have made your position clear. Thank you for your honesty. I am your humble servant,

Mrs. Lavinia Sparks, Chapter President
Teachers Against Class Prejudice (TACP)

"It is a terrible thing to see and have no vision."
Helen Keller

5 / Testing

Miz Sparks, is it true Antipathy got suspended for nothing? That's what everybody's saying.

Yes, Jayan. Antipathy was suspended this morning, but she will return to us shortly. I'm unsure of the reason, but she may have been injudicious with her choice of words.

Does that mean she cursed somebody out?

As I've already stated, Leilani, I'm unclear about precisely what transpired, but I can affirm that "cursing somebody out" would fall into the general category regarding an injudicious use of language.

Antipathy is always cursing somebody out. Damn.

No cursing, Quincy. Fifth graders, I have seen multitudes of your ilk over my long and laborious career, and it has become abundantly clear to me that trying out curse words is the province and delight of children the world over. However, school is neither the time nor the place to indulge that conspicuous pleasure.

Capiche, Miz Spark.

Benissimo. Now, I have a treat for you today, something entirely unplanned.

Is it donuts, Miz Sparks?

No, Kenji, you will not be receiving any donuts from Miz Sparks. I love you far too much for donuts. However, I do have some apples and cheese.

Apples and cheese? Is that all we get?

Oui, De'Andre, des pommes et des fromage.

What's that?

French apples and French cheese, dummy.

How 'bout some French fries, Miz Sparks?

Renard, if you do not wish to partake of apples and cheese, you are welcome to indulge in two parts hydrogen and one part oxygen.

What's that? Air?

That's cold, Miz Sparks.

She said we could eat air.

No, she didn't. She said we could drink water.

Miz Sparks is cold.

For real.

Now, who would like to play kickball?

Me!

Over here, Miz Sparks.

I want to play.

Do we have to play?

Today, it is my earnest intention to teach everyone in this class how to engage in a proper game of kickball.

We already know how to play, Miz Sparks.

Does everyone know how to play, William? A proper game? I find that hard to believe.

We'll show you, Miz Sparks.

I look forward to that, Saida. Please raise your hand if you've never played kickball. Don't be shy. We all have to start somewhere. Very good.

But those are girls, Miz Sparks. They just like to stand around and gossip.

Is that so? What do you think, Elizabeth? Are you going to sit there and take that?

We want to play. The boys won't let us.

Well, today, we're going to take our apples and cheese to the playground for a classroom game of kickball—girls against boys.

We'll kill 'em.

We'll see about that, Renard.

Does Harry have to be on our team?

Harry, how would you like to be captain of the boy's team?

Ah, Miz Sparks, that's cold.

Miz Sparks is a cold, cold woman, my friends.

Miz Sparks, isn't there a new rule against kickball?

Not that I'm aware of, Serena. It's hard to keep up with all the new rules. Gather your things.

I call first.

I call pitcher.

That's not fair.
You always pitch.
I call captain.
Harry is captain, man. 'Cause you had to open your big mouth.
Oh, yeah.
Ikimasho, les enfants.
C'mon, I'll race you.
On your mark, get set, go!
Okay, girls, let's strategize. Our goal is to get on first.
Miz Sparks, you gonna be on our team?
Why, of course, Princess. Miz Sparks was once a girl, you know.
Can we go first?
As a matter of fact, we can, Felicity.
Who's going to pitch?
Anyone who wishes to, Isi, my dear. There's no rule about changing
pitchers, is there?
No, Miz Sparks, but the boys want the ball pitched a certain way.
Well, Claire, they'll have to be patient today, since some of us will be
learning the game.
They're not going to like that.
But they'll benefit from it. And that's my concern, as your teacher.
Patience is a most valuable attribute. Don't you agree, Netanya? And
waiting is a highly useful skill.
Look, Miz Spark, they're already lining up to kick.
You call that a line, Elizabeth? I call that chaos. Fifth graders, before
we start the game, let's enjoy a snack on the benches over there.
Come on. I'll race you.
Look, Miz Spark, here comes Coach.
Hey, Coach, wanna play kickball? Huh?
Ooh, Ms. Sparks, Coach said we ain't supposed to be playin' no kickball.
Who said anything about kickball? We're here to review our knowl-
edge of physics. This is not kickball. It's science.
For real?
For real. Who's ready? Tuan?
I'm ready, Miz Sparks.
Look, Miz Spark, you made Coach laugh.

I call relief pitcher.

There's no relief pitcher in kickball.

Do you see a bullpen?

Who remembers Newton's First Law of Motion?

I do, Miz Sparks. If an object is in motion, it will remain in motion. If an object is not in motion, it will remain not in motion.

Inertia. Very good, Kiana. One point for our team.

That ain't fair, Miz Sparks.

Why not, De'Andre?

I thought we was gonna play kickball.

We are. The girls are leading, 1-0.

Ah, that's messed up.

Indeed. Now, how do you suppose Newton's First Law applies to kickball? Serena?

No fair, Miz Sparks, it's the boys' turn.

I only see girls' hands. Get your hands up, boys. All right, let's see what you've got. Algernon?

It means the ball is just sitting there and it'll keep sitting there unless somebody kicks it.

Good, Algernon. 1-1. What's an example of another kind of force that could cause the ball to move?

Miz Sparks, it's the wind. Air force.

I'll take it, Serena. 2-0.

No, it's not. It's 2-1.

Thank you, Jayan. I stand corrected. Does anyone have another example of a force that could act upon the ball?

The force of my mind.

And what would that be called, Efraím?

Supernatural power.

It's all in your mind, my friend, all in your mind. Women?

Well, it could be electromagnetic force, but it's really more like friction. It's an opposing force.

Excellent, Claire. That's 3-1 for the ladies.

They already got three points? They haven't even touched the ball.

Boys, who can tell me Newton's Second Law of Motion? Let's give someone else a turn, Algernon. You've already had a turn.

That's not fair.

Sure it is, Quincy. Everybody gets one turn at bat. Do you want to give it a try, Pedro?

Can I give my turn to somebody else?

No substitute batters allowed. Newton's Second Law of Motion. Come on, boys.

Miz Sparks, is Newton's Second Law the one where for every action there's an equal and opposite reaction? Like if you kick the ball, I catch the ball.

That's Newton's Third Law, Zachary.

Can we still get a point? We ought to be able to get a point for that.

Fair enough. Girls, can anyone name Newton's Second Law.

I can, Miz Sparks. Newton's Second Law of Motion means when you kick the ball in the air then it starts to come down really fast 'cause of acceleration and the force of gravity and the mass of the ball makes it do that.

I couldn't have put it better myself, Felicity.

We're leading 4-2.

No bragging, Princess.

So what! We're going to kick your Newtons.

Quelle violence, Elijah. Take a deep breath. The girls have more points. Girls up first.

Yeaaaaa!

We bad, we bad, we whupped your ass and made you sad. We bad, we bad . . .

Let's play ball.

Miz Sparks, can you tell them to shut up?

Girls, let's not gloat. Please settle on a kicking order. The old lady goes first.

Who's the first pitcher?

How about someone who has never had the opportunity to pitch before?

But they can't even pitch, Miz Sparks. That's why they don't pitch.

Of course, they can. It's physics. If they use what they know about physics, they'll be just fine. Pitching is both an art and a science.

Is everything science, Miz Sparks?

Yes, Jayan. Everything that isn't art. And some things that are. Now, before we get started, let's establish the rules.

No bunting, Miz Sparks.

That's fine. Are there any other rules I should be aware of?

If there can't be no pinch hitters, then there can't be no pinch runners.

I think we girls can live with that.

But Miz Sparks, I'm not wearing the right shoes.

I can see that, Genevieve. Girls, this is an opportunity to learn a lesson you will need for the rest of your lives. Boys, you listen as well. Proper footwear is essential. Capiche?

Capiche!

Anyone whose footwear is not conducive to running will be obliged to walk the bases. Walking is not as efficient, but it's potentially as successful.

Kenji gets to wheel the bases. Why can't we wheel the bases?

Kenji, are you going to let that slide?

You idiots get to slide the bases. That's why your heads go bump in the night.

Who's got another rule? Saida?

No head balls or foot balls.

How about breast balls?

That's nasty, Miz Sparks.

That's necessary, Pedro.

Okay, no blessed balls. I can't even say it.

How about "no strike outs?"

No strike outs? Miz Sparks!

Because some people are just learning to kick, Tuan. They need the extra pitches.

What about foul outs?

No foul outs, Jayan. Same reason.

Come on, Miz Sparks. They'll be up forever. I mean, if they can't strike out and there's no foul outs or breast balls, how we ever gonna get them out?

Butt balls.

Oooh, Miz Sparks, you said "butt!"

Les boules frappant avec les derrieres. It always sounds nicer to speak of butts in French. Oui, De'Andre?

Who's pitching, Miz Sparks?
Harry is pitching. And this old lady is going first.
He can't pitch.
Why is he pitching?
Check it out.
Miz Sparks can kick.
Catch it, you idiot!
We ain't never gonna get up.
Watch out, Tuan. Here, I come.
She's out.
She's out! I saw it.
I hit her on the pants.
Sorry, no pants balls, Efraím.
This is not fair, Miz Sparks. This is discrimination.
Of the very best kind.
Miz Sparks is cheating.
Oh, phooey. How about a "do-over?"
Miz Sparks, you're cheating for the girls.
I bet that makes you mad, doesn't it, Will?
Hell, yes.

Which is another reason why we're out here today. We need to know what to do and what to say when we're mad. When we're in the middle of a kickball game and we don't agree and the tempers are flaring and steam is beginning to come out of the ears, we need to know how to calm ourselves down. What do you think, Quincy? Does it make more sense to have a "do-over" or to waste a lot of time arguing?

If you're right, then you should argue.

Sometimes, that's true. But are we here to exercise our entire bodies, or only to exercise our mouths?

We see your point, Miz Sparks. Can we get on with the game?

Yes, we can, Zoe. I'm going to stay out of it. Here's what you need to know. Every time you curse or insult someone on your team or on the other team, you'll cost your team a point.

But what if we're just cursing to ourselves?

Then keep it to yourselves, Jayan. Everything that passes through your head doesn't need to come tumbling out of your mouth. Am I right, Renard?

Does "hell" count, Miz Sparks?

Everything counts, Bao. Get used to "phooey."

Oh, man. What the phô?

Get used to "fiddlesticks."

That's corny, Miz Sparks.

That's colorful, Princess.

Uh oh, here comes Major Minor.

I bet Miz Sparks is gonna be in trouble.

How much you wanna bet?

A quarter.

All right. I'll see you and raise you a quarter.

Children, who can tell Major Minor what we're learning in physics?

I can, Miz Sparks. What goes up must come down.

Thank you, Kenji. And I'll tell you what else we're learning, Major Minor. We've figured out that there are many variables that influence the trajectory of the ball. For example . . .

I know, Miz Spark, I know! The type of shoe.

Bueno, Marcus. What else?

The placement of the kick.

Kalós, Jerusalem. What else?

The amount of air in the ball.

Excelente, Elijah. What else?

The direction of the wind.

Bravo, Saida. Anything else?

The friction caused by pebbles on the playground.

Splendide, Omar.

Oh, I get it, Miz Sparks. This is not just science; it's math, too. The angle of your foot to the ball. The curve it makes when it flies. The percentage of hits for each team. Listen up, people. Miz Sparks is trying to teach us something.

I'm sure Major Minor would agree, Xochitl. Students, please share with your families what you learned today.

This was the best day. We didn't learn anything.

I hope you learned something, Quincy.

I know what he means. He means we didn't have to read a book.

But you read the book first. Don't you remember, Bao? We read about Newton's laws, and then we acted them out. Now, who can tell me who Newton was?

Didn't he invent figs?

Very funny, Leilani.

Nah, that was Newman.

Make sure you study for your test tomorrow.

Miz Sparks, is physics everything?

Yes, Jayan, physics is everything.

This has happened before.
The child has been sent home for
days at a time with nothing to do.
Her infractions are too many to
recount. Mrs. Brown hopes the girl
will settle down of her own accord,
but she seems to get worse with each
passing year. Adolescence will soon
be upon them. Oh, dear. Much to fear,
much to fear. Jail, for one thing.
Prison. The chair. Let's not go there.
The kid is only eleven. She
wouldn't be the first Brown the State
had put down at taxpayer expense.
All the Browns, save a few, survive
at taxpayer expense, small recompense
for their centuries of degradation
at the hands of one ungrateful nation.
Antipathy's bad luck was being born
at a time when Americans
were struggling with
"compassion fatigue."

The Browns are fatigued.
Their family history could pass for
an empirical study of unnatural ways
to perish. Brown cousins have been
unwilling participants in every
genocide of the last five centuries.
There were Brown victims of Pizarro—
the Chumpi in the city of Coracora.

The Barnas of Hungary fell siege to
Suleiman. And how many Donnellys
succumbed to the Irish Potato Famine?
That was anybody's guess. Brown Beaver
was murdered at Wounded Knee.
The Moreno family was massacred
by Yankees in the Philippines.
Brunsteins starved to death under Stalin.
The Brauns of Lodz perished at
the Bergen-Belsen concentration camp.
Sure, there was a Brown on the other end
of every sword, but their deeds were unsung,
save for Old John Brown, who was given his
due, both as God's Avenger and His martyr, too.

Don't know Adam's last name, but Eve
was clearly a Brown, if you consider
her unfortunate dealings with the snake,
her woman pains, her one son killing
the other, and all those descendants dying
in that flood. Then all the remaining ones
being taken into slavery, suffering
all manner of abuse in Babylon and
singing their lamentation with as much
conviction as the Brown singers of
Memphis, Tennessee. Yes, Eve
walked through many a storm, and if she
wasn't Black, she was definitely Brown.

Antipathy can recite a litany of loss
on both sides of her family. She knows
who was lynched and who was
drowned, whose breasts
ballooned with tumors the size of pies,
who went the way of the gangs, who
got eaten away by stomach pangs,
who drunk their way and drugged

their way to the far side of oblivion,
who dragged themselves to killer
jobs on factory lines or took breathless
jobs inside of mines, who retired and
died a day later, who went away to
fight a war and was never heard from
no more, who lost the store, the farm,
the shirts off their backs, who died
under attack from someone they loved,
who got shoved from a balcony or
fell down an elevator shaft or was
overcome by a sudden draft or got carried
away by a sudden storm, who met
their Maker before they were born.

Antipathy is proud of her history,
her parents who love her, her shaky
family tree, her mother, Antigone
Tremonisha Brown, who married
Patmos Anthony Brown because she
liked his name. Antipathy was a
Double Brown -- some would say
Brown Squared, double-crossed by
Fate. Her Grandmama Artemis had
acted in many a melodramatic Texas
pageant. (Yes, she had a twin brother
who played a handmade zither.)
Her favorite roles were Antigone,
Ulrica, Cassandra, and Lucretia, hence, the
names of her four daughters. Her sons
were Agamemnon, Orpheus, and
Polyneices. All dogs were either Zeus
or Cupid. Most of the kids had different
dads. Agamemnon came from a very
bad seed. When Uncle Aggy killed
Uncle Poly, it broke Big Mama Artie's

heart. She thought it was her fault for
taking up with his daddy. But just like
Eve, God gave her another child, who
she named Seth, just to be safe.

Antigone spent her childhood raising
her mother's children, so she never
wanted children of her own, but when
she was forty, she met and married
Patmos, who was twenty-seven and
sturdy as an Alabama oak. He sang
real sweet like her Mama, with a voice
just as high. His father was Moses.
His mother was Patrice. His
brothers and sisters—Morice, Matrice,
Posy, Sesom, Sepa, and Cirta—doted on
their baby brother. In some parts (but not in
these parts) he is still called Baby Brown.
Baby Brown is a good friend to men.
He has a special place in his heart
for the relentlessly unemployed.
In good times, they can count on
Alabama hushpuppies and Texas
barbecue. In bad times, they can count
on Mary Jane and Johnnie Walker.

For awhile anyway, Antipathy has never
been treated so well. She enjoys all
aspects of being suspended for no reason:
her parents' outrage, their refusal to make
her do homework, their threatening to hire
a lawyer and take the District to court.
Sometimes, her mother will let her
rest against her arm, something she
hasn't done since she was a young girl.
People visit and encourage her,
but they don't come near her, which

is always her preference but not
always respected until now. Her cousins
are not allowed to tease her, a benefit
for which she is especially grateful.
What's more, she is given things to
pass the time. She's given ice cream,
which she can't eat because it makes
her sick. She's given a deck of cards
with dogs wearing crowns. She's given
wishes from her classmates and blessings
from her church. She's given sympathy,
an entirely new experience. Antigone Brown
prays over her daughter and enlists her
prayer circle to do the same. Something is
wrong, something more than usual. Antipathy
must be getting her monthly, abdomen tender
and bloated, hard to tell what's hurting. She's
drawing a bath when the phone rings.

"Anti, see who that is. Don't answer
unless it has a name, I mean, a good name.
I don't want any Anonymous calling me.
I've had enough of their animosity."
    "It's the school."
    "What do they want? You're
already suspended. Isn't that enough of an
alibi?"
    "Yeah. Uh huh. Whatever. Okay."
    "Whose that on my phone?"
    "It's the principal. She wants to talk
to a parent."
    "Give the phone to your father. He needs
to do some work today."
    "Daddy, it's the principal on the phone."
    "What principal?"
    "At my school."

"How old are you?"

"Don't you remember? I'm eleven."

"Why can't you be done with school, like my other kids? I'm tired of having to pay for your schooling."

"It's free, Daddy."

"Naw, nothing is free. You remember that. They put that tax on candy and pop and the lottery. They find a way to make us pay. Using my taxpayer dollars to harass me at home."

"Do you miss me, Mrs. Camelione?"

"Girl, give me the phone. Hello, this is Patmos Brown. Who's this?"

"She's a liar, Daddy. She said she missed me. Don't believe a word she says."

"What do you mean? You can't extension the suspension. An investigation?"

"What's she saying, Daddy?"

"I beg your pardon. I'd like to talk to the teacher. What do you mean I can't talk to the teacher?"

"Call, Miz Sparks, Daddy. She knows what happened."

"Send a letter home? Don't bother."

"Did you hang up on her, Daddy?"

"That cow is crazy."

"Patmos, what was that all about?"

"She was trying to say there's something wrong with Anti."

"There ain't nothin' wrong with me. Something's wrong with her."

"Don't worry, Little Bit. Daddy's gonna take care of everything. You just wait and see. I'm going to call my lawyer. Two can play at this game."

"Patmos, I know you're not calling that

ambulance chaser from the TV. He got your
hopes up after that fender bender, and you
ended up with another DUI and a suspended
license. There ain't nothin' he can do for you.
Anti, come get in the bath."

"Yes, Mama."

"I'll call Miz Sparks."

"Mama, do you think I can go back to school
next week?"

"I hope so, Baby. I'll call Miz Sparks and see.
In the meantime, you can study the Bible.
Your daddy and I have somewhere to go.
Don't be letting anybody in the door, you hear?"

"Can I read the Bible in the bathtub?"

"What chapter are you on?"

"I'm on the Psalms."

"Good. You read until we get back.
Then, we'll see what you know."

7 / How to Fire a Teacher

The Principal, Agitated

With ring finger she presses paper clip to palm
until a bruise forms along the line of her life.
Her hand she hides beneath the desk. Her doubt
she pours into the cracks crisscrossing the pine
floor of what used to be the nurse's room.
Due to deep cuts, the nurse comes only once
a week. These days, deep cuts are all the rage.
That summer class explaining how to fire
a teacher was well attended. Now the eyes
of conscience glare at her from across the void,
burn a hole in her resolve. Her job is to break
that gaze, to hold it captive as sure as teeth
pinching a tongue, to bend it straight like a thin
piece of metal unfolding at the curves.

The Teacher, Aggrieved

She knows the drill, the twist and curves
of a life in teaching, the moves to thin
the ranks of workers who cut their teeth
on union beer in the days of make or break
strikes about respect. Now the gains are void.
She wishes. From behind a veil of hurt, she eyes
her adversary. Too late to halt or smother the fire
melting her heart or turn the cheek or stifle the rage
gripping her neck or give an inch, just this once.
She slaps her hand on the desk. Used to be room
for dissent. Those who aren't careful might pine
for a past when leaders were strong and doubt
was a sign of courage. She rises to meet her life,
pain as sharp as a nail through her savior's palm.

8 / The Language of Grief

Lavinia and Herman Sparks
ushered at church, played golf
on Saturdays, led Wednesday
night Bible study at the senior
center, reading chapter and
verse to the hard of hearing,
turning wrinkled pages with
arthritic fingers swelling
inside their silver rings.

She didn't like gold,
never had, not since the days
when people were mined for
their fillings. She knew a
woman who sold her gold
to save her house and lost
them both. Oh. But that
golden anniversary, she
would have liked that.

It was not to be. He
had smoked his way through
tragedies, starting with her
breast cancer, steady through
his mother's stroke and his
father's Alzheimer's, and lit up
again after the death of their
only child. Two packs a day,
one right after another.

Friends of her son still
come round. They come
with spouses. She doesn't
mind. Bring their children.
Hard to bear. She longs for
her unknown grandkids, their
warm lips on her cheek, her
fingers in their hair, their
dimples round as water.

Every year, she watches
children rise like stalks of
bamboo. For the teacher,
this is joy. For the parent,
this is heartache of an
everlasting kind. Frozen in
time, bound by circles of
gray, cold as the morning
she lost her boy.

When they found him, he was
bare, fragile as when she first
cradled him, first pressed him
to her chest, first gave him of
herself. He looked as if he'd
been following the moonlight.
He looked as if he'd been
seeking the distant shore of
a long-forgotten lake.

Lavinia and Herman Sparks
treated each other with
kindness. She stroked his
face. He brought himself
closer. They sang many a
faraway hymn, drove
to church holding hands.
But nothing could bring
her back to him.

She was a *sansoleil,*
a parent who lost a child.
She could not accept this grief.
She could not stop blaming
herself. She could not cease
cursing the sky. Her God
hides his face. Each night,
she falls to the earth, a star
in search of fire.

Her breasts ache. Listless
berries that never ripen.
The constant shivering.
A fallen sun. She searches
the empty house, waiting on
benches carved with names.
Keep busy, the widows say.
They only know half her pain.
She is a *sansoleil.*

Section Two
Counter Punches

February

9 / Crispus Attucks Rides Again

Lavinia Sparks rose at dawn to make a final correction to the day's program. It seemed that Crispus Attucks would make an appearance after all. At the very last minute, Antipathy Brown had decided to play the hero of the Boston Massacre, complete with ascot and tri-cornered hat. Her suspension for chewing out the sub had finally ended, and she had once again returned to her fifth-grade classroom, where she seemed content to relive the dawn of the American Revolution.

Miz Sparks had given the American Revolution a certain allure by linking it to the legacies of the Greek, Roman, and Persian empires, the Umayyad Caliphate, the European plague, the Spanish Inquisition, the rise of the Ottoman empire, the horrors of the transatlantic slave trade, the conquests of indigenous peoples, the imperial rivalries among the crowns of England, France, the Netherlands, Portugal, and the very Catholic Spain, the French Revolution, the Haitian Revolution, the Russian Revolution, and the international trafficking in addictive substances. She felt it was her duty to divulge as many secrets as possible in the waning months of fifth grade. Most of her students didn't have two nickels' worth of common sense, and she attributed this flaw to the fact that their entire school careers had been devoted to denying evolution, airbrushing the founding fathers, and ascribing to all manner of propaganda because that's what the experts on the Texas School Board in Austin said they should do. The message that truth was actually verifiable had never been conveyed.

Lavinia didn't really approve of the word massacre to describe what happened in Boston. She reserved the word massacre for the kind of slaughter that occurred at Wounded Knee and Sand Creek. In her mind, what happened in Boston had more in common with Kent State—frightened soldiers shooting at protestors. The fact that Crispus Attucks, a well-dressed and educated Black man, was the first to take a musket shot was just an early example of racial profiling. The British soldiers claimed he had threatened them with a stick. Just another angry Black man with revolutionary leanings. He paid the price.

Now it was her turn to pay the piper. Mrs. Camelione was no redcoat, but she wielded a government issue musket as well as anyone ever had. Whenever she summoned Miz Sparks to the office for her weekly dressing down, her bullet-pointed volleys left the older woman riddled with ire. Menopause had not been kind to Lavinia, especially toward the end of the school day when she lost her ability to fire back.

As she downed her third cup of coffee on what promised to be a very long day, she couldn't help wondering if this would be her last assembly. She was tired. Dog tired. Fried, wired, spent, dazed, and stupefied. Re-re-re-re-re-re-re-retired, that's what she should be. The sad trials of children reminded her of her own lonely circumstances. Sometimes she feared she might be carried away on a river of grief. She vowed to retire before they carried her out in a box. In the meantime, she needed to stay busy. She put on Aretha and danced down the kitchen.

It had been nine months since Herman died. She was still furious with him for leaving her. There, on the turquoise shelves above the kitchen counter, his photo taunted her. Swinging for the fairway in his favorite Lee Elder white golf cap, he had gone to that last tournament without her. They had planned to retire to Greece, where he had once been stationed as a merchant marine. She longed for fishing villages, wildflowers, and men dressed in white. How dare Herman leave her while she could still dance. By the time she sat down at her computer, she had the vim and vigor of a Kennedy.

With the program safely stashed on her thumbdrive, Lavinia was now ready to face the day. She slipped on the gown Jerusalem's father had brought her from Ethiopia, covered her wrists with bracelets made in Senegal, put on her favorite earrings from Tunisia, and wrapped her hair in a scarf purchased on last summer's trip to South Africa. The makeup she kept to a minimum—a hint of rouge, a dash of powder, a slash of lipstick. By the time she reached her classroom, the boots from Israel and coat from Norway had given way to sandals from Brazil and shawl from Brooklyn. She unplugged her car and coasted the five miles to work. Like a spawning salmon, her journey home was entirely uphill.

PROGRAM FOR 32ND AFRICAN AMERICAN HISTORY MONTH ASSEMBLY

Marian Anderson	as played by	Kiana Moore
Canada Lee	"	Zachary Jones, III
Paul Robeson	"	Cynthina Gregory
Dorothy Dandridge	"	Princess Johnson
Angela Davis	"	Claire Davis-Walker
Shirley Chisholm	"	Serena Kruse
Barbara Jordan	"	Saida Mohammed
Frederick Douglass	"	Jayan Patel
Buffalo Soldiers	"	Bao Pham, Tuan Nguyen, Pedro Brayboy, Omar Martinez, Harry Wilson-Clarke, Elijah Ladu
Crispus Attucks	"	Antipathy Brown
Cakewalk Dancers	"	Leilani Lemalu, Jerusalem Tadesse, Isi Edwards, Algernon Metoyer, Felicity Goodwin, Quincy Smith, Genevieve Dumlao, Efraím Rivera, De'Andre Jackson, Elizabeth Yang, Zoe Allen, Netanya Miller-Resnick, Xochitl Hernandez, Will Robinson
Fats Waller	"	Renard Balthazar
Scott Joplin	"	Kenji Takahashi
Dr. James Weldon Johnson, Esq.		Sir Marcus Thompson

Still, she enjoyed arriving. Among her friends, she counted Coach Birdsong, Miss Juanita, most of the teachers and all of the bilingual aides, the women in the cafeteria, the custodian, the mailman, and the crossing guard. Before the assembly started, she would cut the line to the copy machine, elbow past a few colleagues on her way to the teachers' restroom, and pop her head in the office to wish the principal a Happy Lincoln's Birthday. She was decidedly unhappy about Mrs. Camelione's decision to employ the code phrase "Mr. Lincoln is in the building" as a warning whenever dangerous suspects might be roaming the premises. Why not Mr. Booth? In the mornings, Miz Sparks could hold her own.

The principal was not in her office. Much to Miz Sparks's chagrin, she was fiddling with the sound system. They greeted each other like wary cats. Mrs. Camelione announced that the assembly was not to exceed half an hour. Oddly enough, Miz Sparks hadn't anticipated problems with the assembly. Every year, it ran as smoothly as a Swiss watch. Parents and students looked forward to her lively introductions and the students' charming impersonations. Now it seemed as if her role was in doubt.

"I will be giving the welcome," Mrs. Camelione declared, "in order to assure a respectful climate. Please keep your students quiet back stage."

"I'll be doing the introductions."

"I'm afraid we won't have time for those. If the rehearsals were representative, the program is already too long."

"But how will the audience learn the history?"

"It's not possible to learn history from half-hour school assemblies. College is the place for students with an interest in history. That's not our mandate. Elementary school students are too young to understand history."

"I disagree."

"How surprising."

Miz Sparks made her way to the portables. The rouge on her face had spread; she was hot all over. On her way to the classroom, she came across Marcus, dressed in suit, tie, glasses, and mustache.

"Good morning, Dr. Johnson," she greeted him.

"Good morning, Miz Sparks." He handed her a rose.

She hugged him to her. "Are you ready for the assembly?"

"I am, Miz Sparks."

"Very well. Miz Sparks is feeling under the weather. Would you help me by doing the introductions?"

"Are you sure, Miz Sparks? I don't know as much history as you do."

"That's not true. You know everything I've taught you and everything you've taught me, and one day you'll make a fine professor."

"Thank you, Miz Sparks."

"Thank you, Dr. Johnson. Is this rose from your grandmother's garden?"

"No, I bought it from the flower shop. I bought one for you and one for my mother and one for my sister."

"Where did you get the money?"

"Babysitting."

"You're a very kind person."

"I know."

As the other students began to descend upon the portable, Miz Sparks found her mood was lifting. If this class were to be her last, she would leave knowing her career had been a success, Antipathy notwithstanding. Or maybe because of Antipathy, who mirrored her own inner warrior, she could find the strength to face her disenchantment. In many ways, Lavinia Sparks was still a fifth-grade child wanting the world to be fair.

She looked around the room. There was Marian (Kiana) Anderson dressed in a long purple gown, hair pressed and parted on the side, heels dangerously high. Next to her stood a remarkably composed buffalo soldier, whose grandma had taken him to a store that sold Australian cowboy clothes. Admiring, protective, Pedro hung on her every note. He wasn't the only one. In her circle of illustrious friends, Marian could count Canada (Zachary) Lee, Shirley (Serena) Chisholm, and Kenji (Scott Joplin) Takahashi, all dressed in her husband's suit jackets, which Miz Sparks had tailored to fit. Serena was vintage Shirley in a wide collar 70s geometric print. Her oversized eyeglasses went perfectly with her costume.

But by far, the person who moved her most was Genevieve Dumlao, lovely as a cuckoo dove in her grandmother's pantomina skirt. The kid's life had been no cakewalk. She and her mother had been airlifted out of the Manila slums by a second cousin from Canada who had managed to make a small fortune selling orchids. Wearing a cerise orchid stem as a barrette, she made her way in a country of comparatively well-off classmates. Next to her, Efraím shimmied and shined, resplendent in his white *guayabera.*

"Fifth graders, you look marvelous. Let's prance over to the auditorium, arm in arm, two-by-two, tall and straight. Onward, Buffalo Soldiers." Miz Sparks had been turning this same phrase for thirty-two years.

Nathaniel had been her original buffalo soldier. Ever since he was a toddler, he had taken care with his clothes. By the time he was in her class, he was already ironing his jeans. He did all the family ironing—her dresses, his father's shirts. She thought he might join the military, once he finished school. But instead, he went off to Jamaica with his childhood friends—the original Tuskegee airman, the original Harlem Hellcat, and the original infantryman from the 54th Massachusetts. The Berlin Wall had been dismantled, piece by piece, the film *Glory* had just been released, and the Persian Gulf War had yet to begin. All of the boys wanted to be soldiers.

She could still see him prancing to the head of the line. The blue uniform, his yellow scarf, black boots, white gauntlets still rested in the back of his closet, as crisp and creased as the last day he ironed them. Before his fifth grade year was over, he joined a local troop and wore that same uniform every week until he finally outgrew it at the age of fifteen. By then, all his friends had gone off to girls. As shy as he was short, Nathaniel had only started courting girls right before he died. Eighteen and lanky in khaki dress pants, he would leave the house carrying flowers from his father's rose garden. He never told his mother any of his girlfriends' names. She could only guess who among the weeping young strangers who came to his funeral might have known his heart.

Her class waited quietly backstage for the principal to finish the welcome speech. For the first time in thirty-two years, Miz Sparks did not wait with them. She sat in the audience next to Coach Birdwell, back straight, eyes forward, chest out, knees fastened, feet together, gaze cast in the distance.

Mrs. Camelione finished with a challenge: "And so, my fellow lifelong learners: Ask not what your District can do for you; ask what you can do for your District." A loud gasp emanated from the parent chairs. Gloria Moore snapped a picture of the podium, which the PTA had draped in Kente cloth. Queenie Johnson's phone rang. The kindergarteners whispered sweet nothings while the sixth graders told dirty jokes. Finally, it was time for Marcus.

"Everybody please rise for the African American National Anthem, which I, Dr. James Weldon Johnson, wrote all the way back at the turn of the last century. It will be sung for you today by Marian Anderson, fresh from her concert at the Lincoln Memorial. Go, Marian."

> *Lift every voice and sing*
> *till Earth and Heaven ring,*
> *ring with the Harmony*
> *of Liberty.*

"Please join in, everybody. Marian can't carry this all by herself."

> *Let our rejoicing rise*
> *high as the list'ning skies.*
> *Let it resound*
> *loud as the rolling sea.*

"That's better, people. Now, I want you to lift e-ver-y voice."

> *Sing a song*
> *full of the faith that the dark past has taught us.*
> *Sing a song*
> *full of the hope that the present has brought us.*

"Beautiful. Keep going."

> *Facing the rising sun*
> *of a new day begun,*
> *Let us march on*
> *till Victory is won.*

"Thank you, Marian. Let's give her some snaps. Please remain standing for the school pledge, which will be led by actors Canada Lee . . .

> *Merciful powers!*
> *Restrain in me the cursèd thoughts that nature*
> *Gives way to in repose.*

" . . . Paul Robeson,

> *Go down, Moses, way down to Egypt land.*
> *Tell ole Pharaoh to let my people go.*

"And who are you? Dorothy Dandridge. Take it away, Dorothy."

> *Loves a baby that grows up wild*
> *He don't do what you want him to.*
> *Love ain't nobody's angel child*
> *He won't pay any mind to you.*

"Okay, on the count of three. One-un, two-oo, three-ee. Everybody!"

> *We'll float like a butterfly,*
> *Sting like a bee*
> *All the way to Victory!*

"Please be seated. Is Crispus Attucks in the house? Has anybody seen Crispus? Okay, then, let's give it up for Angela Davis, Shirley Chisholm, and Barbara Jordan. Come on, y'all, everybody's waiting."

> *Service is the rent that you pay for room on this earth.*

"Thank you, Representative Chisholm."

> *We know the road to freedom has always been stalked*
> *by death.*

"Thank you, Professor Davis."

> *Do not call for Black power or green power. Call for brain*
> *power.*

"Thank you, Congresswoman Jordan. Let's give them a hand. Is that Crispus Attucks I see? He must be going the other way. Please welcome the Buffalo Soldiers for a hip-hop version of Bob Marley's popular anthem. Ride on, Soldiers."

> *Stolen from Africa,*
> *Brought to America,*
> *Fighting on arrival,*
> *Fighting for survival,*

"Why, look who's come by to say hello. Mr. Frederick Douglass. Mr. Douglass, do you have something you'd like to say to the American people?"

> *What, to the American slave, is your 4th of July? I answer: a day that reveals to him, more than all other days in the year, the gross injustice and cruelty to which he is the constant victim. To him, your celebration is a sham—a thin veil to cover up crimes which would disgrace a nation of savages.*

"Thank you, Mr. Douglass. Wise words, wise words, my man. Can I get an amen? Can I get an Amen? Thank you, Sister Marian. I, James Weldon Johnson, am a preacher. And I say to you young men and young women gathered here today:

> *Your arm's too short to box with God.*

"That's right. You heard me."

> *Listen! Listen!*
> *All you sons and daughters of Pharaoh*
> *Who do you think can hold God's people*
> *When the Lord God himself has said,*
> *Let my people go?*

"Can I get another Amen?"

> *And Moses lifted up his rod*
> *Over the Red Sea;*
> *And God with a blast of his nostrils*
> *Blew the waters apart.*

"But that ain't all."

> *'Cause I feel Old Earth a-shuddering*
> *And I see the graves a-bursting*
> *And I hear a sound,*
> *A blood-chilling sound.*
> *What sound is that I hear?*
> *It's the clicking together of the dry bones,*
> *Bone to bone—them dry bones.*

"Dry bones! Everybody stand up. Mr. Fats Waller is here to lead us in the traditional version of a little song I wrote called 'Dem Bones, Dry Bones.'

> *Ezekiel cried, "Dem dry bones!"*
> *Ezekiel cried, "Dem dry bones!"*
> *Ezekiel cried, "Dem dry bones!"*
> *Oh hear the word of the Lord.*
> *The foot bone connected to the leg bone,*
> *The leg bone connected to the knee bone,*
> *The knee bone connected to the thigh bone,*
> *The thigh bone connected to the back bone,*
> *The back bone connected to the neck bone*
> *The neck bone connected to the head bone*
> *Oh hear the word of the Lord!*

"Thank you, everybody. You've been a great audience. Does anybody know if Crispus Attucks is going to show up for the revolution?"

Shut up, Marcus. Who told you to do the introductions?

"I knew Crispus was in here somewhere. Ladies and gentlemen, back from the dead, it's Crispus Attucks. What have you got to say for yourself, Mr. Ass...Attucks?"

"I ain't saying nothin'. I'm gonna sing."

"Take it away, then. We can't wait all day."

> *Everybody sit down. I got somethin' to say.*
> *Even though people are dead, it don't mean they're*
> *all the way gone.*
> *I just wanted to say that.*
> *Now, I'm gonna sing, but nobody sing along.*
> *My country 'tis of thee,*
> *sweet land of Liberty,*
> *of thee I sing,*
> *land where my doggie died,*
> *land where my mama cried,*
> *from ever-re-ee mountain side,*
> *le-et chipmunks sing.*

I'm leaving.
It stinks in here.

"And now, the moment everybody has been waiting for . . . our 32nd Annual Cakewalk! Mr. Scott Joplin will play his 'Maple Leaf Rag.' Beam us up, Scottie. This has been the 32nd African American History Month Assembly presented by Miz Sparks' fifth-grade class. Here come the Cakewalk Dancers. Put your hands together."

If that had been the end of it, Miz Sparks would have counted herself among the blessed. As it was, she was forced to stay in for recess, while Cynthina completed her version of the epilogue, which the principal had demanded of every fifth grader.

> *This is what happen when the asembley was almost over krispis attacks yells it stinks in here so he levees to get some fresh air but on the way out he runs into mr lincoln who aint sposed to be here so then he starts yelling mr lincoln is in the bilding and everybody no what that mean so coach birdsong he come running but mr lincoln he got a gun and since the sequity garde got cut and the wakie takies got broke and the nurse miss fine is missing and the cowslur he quit and nobody no where the vice principal stay and miss waneeta loss her voice agin and there was a glich in the sistim its a good thing krispis was in the rong place at the rite time cuz nobody seen mr lincoln at first since he had shave his beerd but then when he snach fats everybody new that was his real daddy who aint never even spose to show his mug up in this mug so krispis attacks led the buffalo soljers and bob marley was singing then barbra jordon made the resque of fats waller but really it was when angela davis raise her fist for black power just as mr lincoln be pasing by and hit him on the chin that the cops cot mr lincoln tring to excape in his brokedown ford on washington street and now he back in jail where he live and this is paul robeson reporting life from muhammad ali.*

Miz Sparks collected the paper, gave Cynthina her blessing and released the girl to play. She read over Cynthina's account and deemed it an accurate description of the alleged events. Like the rest of her students, Cynthina had spent her entire school career journaling instead of composing because that's what the experts in Manhattan said she should do. Somehow, the idea that writing was a formal pursuit requiring a certain attention to rules had not been conveyed. There was no way Miz Sparks could retire while the writing curriculum was still so very ugly.

She put her head on her desk and cried.

Did your tomatoes come in good this year?
Incredible. By the bus loads. We've got tomato sauce, stewed tomatoes, tomato chutney, sun-dried tomatoes, tomato salsa, tomato juice, tomato soup . . . We've got tomatoes.
How about apricots? I like that apricot jam you made two years ago. The one with the cloves.

•

What does she want us to do?
Discuss our strategies for getting kids who don't know English to pass the standardized test from hell.
Again?
That was a different principal.

•

We need to meet about the twins.
What's their story?
They're destroying my classroom.
You've got both of them?
Uh huh.
How did that happen?
You tell me.
You must have done something awful in a previous life.
Or y'all made a mistake with the class assignments.
Us? Made a mistake? Unlikely. Their mother must have insisted upon their God-given right to torment the same person.
Since when do parents run this school?
Since we lost our security guard.
I've had it with all this capitulation.
No use bringing out the big words. Everyone knows you're the only one who can handle those two little devils. You know it, too.

They need to be in a classroom for behaviorally disturbed peewees.
Oh, come on now. How old are they? 5? 6? They're too young to be separated.
And I'm too old to be incarcerated.
Gives me chills just thinking about it.
Lord, save me from your creations.
Just let me know when and where you want me. I'll be there.

•

What did you think about this year's assembly?
That Marcus Thompson is something.
Isn't his mom real young?
And real determined. I've never seen anybody work so hard to give her child everything she didn't have herself. Bless her heart.
Where is the pizza? I heard a rumor she was buying pizza for the whole staff.
The pizza is for after the meeting.
You mean, we have to stay till the end of the meeting to get some lousy pizza? Ain't that nothin'?

•

Where's Coach? Did you notice him and Nurse Fine conspicuously missing from this morning's assembly?
Yeah. Where was he when we needed him?
And did you notice that worthless Minor was nowhere to be found, either?
Sometimes I actually feel sorry for Mrs. Camelione. But only when Mr. Lincoln is in the building.
When Mr. Lincoln is in the building, I feel sorry for us all.
Is she serious? Did she actually say, "It's not important if they get the right answer?" What's more important in math than precision? We're supposed to raise test scores, but it's not important if they get the right answer? Jeez Louise. For the Love of God.

•

When can you meet about the twins?
The 32nd of Juvember is a good day for me.
I am not amused.
I see that. How about next Thursday right after school?
Thank you. Next Thursday in my classroom.
Are they going to be there?
Yes, as long as their mother is there.
Shouldn't we meet at the Hyatt, then? They've got those glass walls for climbing and that oversized chandelier to swing from and that nifty bar with the goblet martinis.
Lord, give me strength.

•

Did she really say we need to double the time we devote to readin', 'riting, and 'rithmetic? What about science? What about social studies? Jeez Pullease. Those subjects are not on the test. That's it, isn't it? She only wants us to teach what's on the test. Kill me now.

•

Are you an organ donor? I'm trying to decide whether or not to be an organ donor.
What you gonna do with them after you're gone?

•

I'm sick of the achievement gap. It's time to get rid of it.
How about a "money gap"? Would you like that better?
Well, that would be apt. How can we compete without money?
Look at the Samoan football players. They don't have money but you can't beat 'em.
That's football. The rules stay the same. But the tests keep changing.
How about a "skills deficit"?
If our kids started passing the tests, they'd have to make new tests.
How about a "competitive disadvantage"?
They should let me create a new test. Listen up. If Cunegunda has 99 cents in the bank . . .

The piggy bank?
And nothing in the mattress . . .
What about her bra? Does she have anything in her bra?
Only flesh, my friend, only flesh.
Continue on, then.
And the light bill is 43 dollars and 11 cents . . .
Let there be light.
How much money does she need to borrow from her cousin Salomea?
That's easy—$5,000.
I'm not finished, yet.
All right. Let me hear the rest of it.
To get the laundry done before they turn off her electricity?
Five thousand dollars and a lot of quarters.
You've got to pick a, b, c, or d.
But what if Cunegunda needs a, b, c, and d?
That's irrelevant.
I'm sticking with my answer. She can't be taking her laundry on the bus.
She needs a car.

•

Are you an organ donor?
No. I don't believe in it. I mean, I might try to sell them, but I'm not giv-
ing them away.

•

Okay, try this one:

If Big Mama is 12 years older than Little Mama and Little Mama has
three kids by the time she's 16, where's Big Daddy?

> a. Prison
> b. The Big House
> c. Down River
> d. In Bed, Sleeping
> e. On the Corner, Drinking
> f. Running for Office
> g. At the Park with the Kids
> h. At Large

That's easy. None of the above. Big Daddy is in a novel that's about to become a movie.
Touché.

•

Have you met the new reading specialist? He says he doesn't work with kids.
Then what good is he?
Beats me. He only works with teachers.
We already know how to read.
He's here to help us teach the kids better.
Another one? He can't teach kids himself, but he's going to help us?
Apparently.
How much do you think they're paying him?
Me and you together. At least.
Unbelievable. Why don't they just hire an assistant teacher that the two of us can share?
That might be really effective. Ain't gonna happen.

•

Writing is not like walking. Is she kidding? It's more like learning to play the violin. You don't clap for a child who's failing violin. It's painful. You teach that kid how to hold the instrument correctly, how to position the bow, the proper fingering, you know, it's complicated. So, let me get this straight. She wants us to improve their writing, but she wants us to clap no matter how poorly they write. Jeez Maneeze.

•

Are you an organ donor?
Of course. Aren't you?

•

Are you free next Thursday? We need to have a meeting about the twins.
Let me get back to you. I left my calendar in my classroom.
Lord, today.

•

Have you met the new counselor?
What happened to the old counselor?
He probably lost his mind.
I doubt it. All he did was fill out paperwork.
Poor guy. They had him running around in circles.
Well, you can't do anything unless the parents sign off on counseling.
The ones who need counseling most don't believe in it.
Do you think the new counselor can make any headway?
Maybe. She's a marathon runner. She might be able to run the circles
faster.

•

Are you an organ donor? I'm trying to decide.
*Take my advice. If they let you pick which organs you want to donate, that
would be one thing. You could say, "Take my eyes, just leave my brain."
But the whole thing is too general. They can take your heart, liver, kid-
neys. I mean, what's to stop them from taking your toes?*
Have you seen my toes?

•

Did you hear she's trying to get rid of Lavinia?
The nerve.
If she gets Lavinia, no telling who'll be next.
Probably Coach Birdsong. He doesn't pay her any mind.
We better lay low.
You've got that right.

•

What's with the picture of the sex offender?
I don't see anything wrong with it.
Suppose the parents see it.
*I think she should send it out to all the parents. So they can be on the look
out for him.*
It's just going to make them panic.

Me, I would want to know if there was a sex offender living across the street from my child's school. She's covering all the bases.

Do other schools do this?

Does it matter what other schools do?

It puts our school in a bad light.

I don't think so. I think it makes it clear that we care about our kids.

But how's a picture of one offender supposed to help them? We need to teach them about behaviors, not scare them with faces. They may have sex offenders living in their houses.

In that case, the picture might help them make the connection.

How is a picture of a Black sex offender going to help a child from Asia? It's just going to reinforce their stereotypes.

If the brother is guilty, he's guilty. Why are you trying to defend him?

He went to this school, that's why. He's an alum.

Don't take it personal. All criminals went to school somewhere.

•

Are you an organ donor?

Believe me. Nobody wants these organs.

•

She's going after Lavinia.

She's wasting her time. Lavinia has more tenure than a Supreme Court justice.

Doesn't matter. That's what this new curriculum stuff is all about. She knows the old teachers won't go for it. She can say they're not doing their jobs, get rid of them, and bring in some timid young weasels for a third of the price. That's the corporate way, baby. Wake up and smell the sleaze.

Unbelievable.

•

Are you an organ donor?

Sure. They're just going to throw them away, you know.

Really?

Don't you watch TV?

•

Do you know about Lavinia?
You mean, about her husband?
No, I mean about her job.
Is she retiring?
No, Camelione is trying to fire her.
Again?
That was another principal.

•

Did I hear that right? Did she really say, 'I want all the side conversations to stop'? Who does she think she's talking to? The kids?

•

I hear she's trying to force Lavinia to retire.
Well, truth be told, it's time for Lavinia to retire. We can all see how unhappy she is.
But what would she do?
That's a good question. I can't imagine her doing anything else.
And what would we do without her?

•

Is that the pizza? I smell pizza.
That's warm cardboard you're smelling.
Oh, no. Don't tell me she got the cheap kind.
She got the kind we feed the kids.
From the cafeteria?
Worse than the cafeteria. The pizza party pizza.
Warehouse pizza?
Warehouse pizza would be a step up. This is that double coupon free delivery pizza.
I thought they went out of business.
Apparently not.
Well, I'm too hungry to complain.
And you'll be too sick to come in tomorrow.
Is that a bad thing?

•

Who put that picture of the sex offender on the door to the teacher's room?

Who do you think?

Why would we want a picture of a sex offender on the door to the teacher's room?

So we can be on the look out for him, you dummy.

Well, he can't be the only sex offender who lives near the school. Why didn't she put up pictures of the white sex offenders and the yellow sex offenders and the red sex offenders and the brown sex offenders? How come she only put up a picture of the black sex offender?

Maybe, she finds him especially offenderish.

Well, I'm offended. I'm tired of the criminal rap. I mean, it doesn't even say what grade he is. Is he a number 1, 2, or 3 sex offender? Is he a flasher or a rapist?

What does it matter? You're a mandatory reporter. Just call the police if you see the guy.

•

Where did they find her?

I hear she's got a few file cabinets of complaints downtown.

They must have sent her here to shut us down.

Or to get rid of her.

You know, those white parents at Rachel Carson didn't put up with her lunacy.

Where was she before that?

Mark Twain. Don't you remember? She was the vice principal over there when that parent tried to get Huck Finn taken out of the library.

That was a whole lot of drama. Who even reads Huck Finn anymore?

Lots of people.

Not in elementary school. That's a high school book.

Well, they had it in the library at Mark Twain.

Go figure.

We've got The Autobiography of Malcolm X and I Know Why the Caged Bird Sings.

Prostitutes, lesbians, all manner of sex offenders. Where will it end?
Harry Potter. He's the Antichrist.
Maybe they should name a school after him.

•

Are you an organ donor?
I'm a cadaver.
Are you planting bulbs this spring?

They sent Incompetence to judge me.
Won't let that joker budge me, no
drudge me, no smudge on my record so
far, I'm a star, always been. One false
evaluation from a failed administration
doesn't scare me. Don't dare me to
expose who they are—with their no-
count facility and low-count virility,
no accountability from powers that
appear to be hostile to me and to my
profession. Pardon the expression:
Life's a stitch in time. The thirty-
five year itch, can't catch it or I'll
scratch it 'fore I die in this ditch. When
she strolls into my room, we're sipping
Three Cups of Tea on a Silk Road
Journey through World History. She
asks me, "How come the backpacks
aren't all hanging up? And how come
these children aren't all sitting down?
Who were those ones I saw running
around without supervision?" Oh, they
had my permission to take a lap around
the playground so their lungs could
expand. Have you noticed the odor
fouling up the land? "Don't try to
distract me. Whatever you're doing
isn't part of the plan. I can have you
removed for endangering your students
by giving them a breather." I'm afraid
what you're saying doesn't make me a

believer. You canceled our recess so
we could work harder, but all of that
work hasn't made us any smarter. The
curriculum you gave us was designed
by idiots. Piteous. What garage sale did
you get it at? An even dozen for a dime?
It must have been the same one that sold
us subprime. Is it a wonder our children
can no longer do the math. Wall Street
can't either. But somehow they get away
with it, don't have to work a day for it.
The rest of us will pay for it. Do the math.
We was robbed, we was cheated, we was
ruthlessly deceited. But what do I know?
I'm nothin' but an honest schoolteacher
without a lot of dough. A bundle of lies
can get you six figures, but don't you
ever wish for an honest living? Why are
you so forgiving of our mis-education in
this first-class nation? The whole place
is at risk, not just our school or our town.
Those heartless bastards will bring us all
down. And I'm sure you know as well as
I do, catching Shanghai is all pie in the sky.
Let's stop foolin' ourselves, stop pullin'
wool over our eyes. While some people I
know like to pretend they don't have any
cousins, I still have dozens, and when they
call me in need, I've been known to gather
speed, even circumvent my sleep to take care
of my peeps. I can't leave 'em. That's the

reason for the gap in our achievin', all
those cousins, all that sufferin', do you
think we can ignore it? Used to be we
could see every person for their talents.
Now we're drowning, out of balance, tied
down like some kind of injured freighter
while some deal negotiator, some progress
negater who goes by the name of Mister
Lowest Common Denominator, makes off
with our senses, our sole inheritances. No,
we're not all on the same page. These days,
techno everything is all the rage. But isn't
floating still basic to learning how to swim?
Isn't balance still needed for riding a bike?
Is it really advisable for every little tike to
learn how to drive, just to stay alive in this
new old economy? Can we teach them how
to switch from their left to their right before
they learn to use a stick shift? I'm finished
being polite to you artificial types who don't
give a holy damn about real people's plight.
"Are you done, Mrs. Sparks? I didn't
come to listen to your crackpot theories or
your pointless criticisms. I'm here to measure
your deliverables and rate your data, evaluate
your progress toward positive outcomes, not
practice my patience and praise your witticisms.
Go on and laugh, but I guarantee you nobody
needs to know about silk. Teachers of your
ilk will soon all be retired, since you can't all
be fired without prolonged and bloody battles.

Why do you always try to rattle me? I'm just
doing my job and demanding you do yours.
Stop teaching about Pakistan. Aren't they our
enemy? Why confuse the children?" Dear
Mrs. Camelione, there are wars going on,
and the students we're teaching were not
even born when the Towers were struck. Can
I show you to the map? Would you like a few
facts about Alexander, Genghis Khan, and the
9/11 attacks? "Miz Sparks, please enlighten me
as to why you're teaching about the world and
its ways when you should be teaching the new
vocab curriculum called Words Their Way?
And you may as well stay mute about your
Greek and Latin roots. I've heard them all
before. Please don't try to be cute. There
are no special favors. Your children need
a serious reboot. They can cut out tiny
strips of paper like the rest of the school.
You're supposed to be teaching the c-k
unit. Duck, truck, trick, stick, stuck, muck,
never mind the rest. Geography and History
aren't even on the Test, so give them a rest.
If you know what's best, you'll bring your
students back on the path with Everyday Math."
Why would I do that? When going to Singapore
for math will take us twice as far, and we'll still
have time to visit Kandahar? "I'll see you in
my office." She leaves in a huff. Tough. I'm
not sure she could find her way to San Jose,
let alone to Palestine. Nor is she inclined

to know the difference between K2 and K9.
She's the K2 of K9s, *canis familiaris*
chasing her tail to no notable avail, yet,
she's determined to prevail and will never
take a rest until and unless she hounds me
to death. I figure her stress is all due to the
Test, but that's no excuse for trying to cook
my goose or spread around the blame for
District policies so lame that they only
accentuate the faulty philosophy and
legendary atrophy that's always brought
to bear when funding is rare. I wouldn't
rent a tent from the current superintendent.
He reeks of indifference, don't try to deny it.
I can definitely see why someone like you
might buy into his lies. No surprise. How
else can you rise when the man personifies
all that is wrong with our sacred institutions?
He's a genuine flack, in open collusion with
the phony prosecution drummed up by the
bloated aiming to go back to the days they
could graze on other people's sorrow, and
slow down tomorrow, stop us from hoping.
Why else would he send an impressionable
like you after a professional like me?
Speaking of bullies, should we pause,
perhaps, and take a moment to appreciate
a girl named Antipathy, who keeps gay
bashers straight? They don't dare mess
with Pedro, not while she's around. She
defends that kiddo against the cruel, my

whole class does, but the same isn't true
for the rest of the school. When he rides
the bus every morning, it's *carte blanche,
laissez-faire,* in-your-face, we don't care.
Is that your win-win situation? Let me
guess . . . it's the game you play best. Blame
it on the teacher when the kids don't act
right. We can always impeach her. She'll go
down without a fight, instead of demanding
the case be airtight. Well, if that's what
you're after, you're barking up the wrong
tree. With the blessing of the District and
the backing of the State and the judgment of
the Mayor that needs to be replaced, no
wonder we're not doing so great. It's the
mission, the vision, not the lack of supervision
but a spate of bad decisions, divisions. Why
do I need your permission to open up the minds
of my innocent victims? No Child Left Behind
and other vacuus dictums don't add up to much
when the teachers go missing. Low retention is
for real, yet we're treated like amateurs by the
saboteurs, provocateurs who couldn't pass a
fifth-grade test. Maybe ignorance is best.
A knowledgeable citizenry, smart voters,
not emoters who it's easy to mislead.
Why read? Separation of church and state
wasn't really what the Founders meant.
They told us their intent. If he didn't
mean it, why would George Washington
have written "In God We Trust" on the

dollar? I'm no scholar, but I've seen it with
my own eyes. No room for compromise.
Let's do away with public schools, libraries,
and swimming pools, those pesky rules and
regulations, foreign trade, the forest service,
immigration, treaties, the United Nations,
roads and beaches, government workers . . .
Did I mention teachers? A worthless lot!
No taxes for anything but defense. Let's
privatize the Army. Spare no expense.
We can save by sending to an early grave
PBS, NPR, NEA, ADA, FDA, EPA, FAA,
FEMA, OSHA, NASA, the CDC, USPS –
all have to go. National Parks, Civil Rights,
Peace Corps, Clean Air, too. What good
do they do? Legal aid, public defenders,
impartial jurists, food stamps, housing for
seniors, passports for tourists? Why leave
the country when it's a jungle out there?
Forget the General Welfare. Justice
is Established over my dead body. Give
me my guns and say your prayers. The
Blessings of Liberty aren't meant for
us *all*. Domestic Tranquility? Code for
Gay Marriage. Can't fool me. Posterity
is limited. If I recall, Sally Hemings's
kids weren't part of the will. No deal.
Proposition 13 was vengeance real.
"Please have a seat. This won't take
long. It's my duty to inform you that
I do not intend to renew your contract

for next year. Do I make myself clear?"
No surprise. I didn't expect otherwise
from the kind of person who parks in
wheelchair spots before leaping from
her SUV with a spring in her step or
honks at old ladies, of which I am one
or yells at grandmas with grandbabies,
of which I have none. Am I just an
obstacle in your rearview mirror?
You look kind of disappointed. Your
face is disjointed, discolored, displeased.
You weren't expecting weeping? Were
you expecting me to go without a fight?
I'll surely be meeting with my union rep
tonight. I've got him on speed dial, yes,
you heard me right. It may require some
legal intervention to get your attention.
I've been asking you to visit since the
beginning of this year. Now it's almost
March, and you suddenly appear to tell
me that my kids are out of control? Do
you mind if I ask: What's your role?
First of all, my kids are fine, with
several notable exceptions, but without
any help, what am I supposed to do?
They have nothing to gain from the likes
of you. If I send them to the office, you
send them right back. Are you trying to
undermine me? Is it really worth that?
I'm just keen to do my job with the
consent of the governed, notwithstanding

their right to be dull and mean. They need
adult guidance. But where have you been?
When I asked for your support to start a
chess club, you shook your head instead,
and I quote, "I can't spend the dough
because I can't recoup it. I can't sell tickets
to a chess club tourney. We only sponsor
sports that require a gurney, so says our
attorney, as long as the parents sign away
their rights to complain, then we're in the game."
You admonish the children not to say
the word "can't," but it's clearly your
favorite. Save it. We bought our own
chess sets, so we can compete with the
college crowd, you should be proud.
But what of all the bus drivers with the
masters degrees? Don't they contribute
to this economy? Does an unemployed
chemist make the same salary as an
unemployed cellist busking Bach in the
subway, down on one knee? Now I'm all
for college, but do we have to sell it by
dissing the mechanics, the chefs, and
electricians? College math for every
man, woman, child. Why is that? So the
jobs will come back from India and China?
Can we find them on a map? Why not tell us
the Truth? The jobs aren't coming back, no
matter how much math we try to cram into
our minds. It's just simple addition, a case of
brutal nonfiction, painfully clear that it's far

away cheaper to bring workers over here.
When it comes to engineers, we're out of our
sphere, and we'll always be behind unless we
once again find a way to teach basic skills.
Unlike China, we gave up all the drills.
You ain't need yo' maf fax. We'll give you
credit for you' effort, tho' yo' solution
ain't worf jack. When the Test comes along
and you don't know what to do cuz you can't
tell the diff'rence 'tween waz false and waz
true, you should just try your best. It can't hurt
to second guess. You're under constant duress
to even out the score, but if you never have to
know anything for good, not the fifty states or
five Great Lakes or how to tell the time, how
to memorize a line of poetry, come up with
a rhyme, identify a native species, formulate a
credible thesis, you'll just keep recalculating
eight times six and six times eight, when the
the answer is the same as it was yesterday.
Isn't that great? Sorry, too late. All those
years you were told to guess-as-you-go cuz
speling don't cownt, well, I hate to sew doubt,
but you were sold a bill of goods. Worry, you
should, but don't bother the School Board, 'cause
they've got other fish to fry. They can multiply.
Money equals clout and we haven't got any.
No penny, no pound, no million dollar bill.
"Are you finished, Miz Sparks? I've got some
things I need to do. You may not be done, but
I'm altogether through." With me? Listen up.

Let me give it to you straight: I'm a first-rate
teacher, and we're hard to come by. We aren't
created in a lab or a graduate class, and we don't
respond kindly to teacher rehab. We're brave
and we're loyal to our students, that's who.
We fight a battle royale to prepare them for life,
show them how to deal with strife, sharpen their
skills, focus their minds. We're advocates, not
missionaries. But a few long decades of
bad policy can make a disillusioned teacher
out of almost anybody. A good teacher can't
rescue poor methodology or steer a rudderless
ship that's headed in the wrong direction on
a test-obsessed trip, no more than a good
actor can redeem a lousy script. We try our
best, now what more can we do? You know,
there's nothing quite so good as a very good
teacher. No simple recipe can produce such
a creature, oddballs often, individuals, yes,
passionate, scary even, liable to stray from
the beaten path, over the line, over the top,
smart, susceptible to reason, and although
this might be treason, I'll say it anyway:
sometimes, the new and improved ain't
all that. Skills, concepts, problem solving—
they all keep the wheels turning, but
skills are the fulcrum, practice, the spokes.
"Thank you, Miz Sparks. Be so kind as to
leave your grades for the quarter in my box.
And don't forget your student narratives. The

substitute starts next Monday. We'll send
a letter to the parents. Until then, I suggest
you take a holiday in lieu of vacation pay.
We'd like to have a clean break, for the
children's sake. I'm afraid I have to go.
So, if you'll just sign on the line, I won't
take any more of your time."

I respectfully decline.

12 / Camelione v. Sparks: *Round 2*

To Lavinia Sparks, 5th Grade Teacher:

Let this letter serve as official notice that you will be placed on official leave beginning March 1st if you refuse to immediately comply with my instructions regarding student discipline, appropriate curricula, and evidence-based best practices in teaching methodology. Let me remind you that all teachers serve at my discretion. While the District may be prepared to honor your contract, it need not be at this school.

Furthermore, I insist that you cease to interfere with our process for choosing a new name for this location. I have already bowed to parent wishes that the naming process be open to school families. I'm not sure what else I can do to ensure that the new name will satisfy all stakeholders. The faculty deadline to submit a name other than Barack Obama or Colin Powell was last Friday.

In addition, it has come to my attention that several students in your class have recently been seen loitering outside the nurse's office. The nurse can see only one student at a time, and the other classes seem to be aware of this rule: If you go to see the nurse and she is with someone else, you wait in the chair outside her office. If someone else is already waiting in the chair, you put your name on the clipboard and return to your classroom.

In contravention to these rules, your students have been sitting on the floor, roaming the hallway, blocking the entrance to the office, and in one case, prostrate in the middle of the hall. This is not a sustainable situation. Your students have to follow the rules, just like everybody else. From now on, anyone who is caught loitering, pass or no pass, will lose their nurse privileges and will be assigned to recess detention for the following day.

Please acknowledge receipt of this letter by leaving a signed copy in my mailbox.

Ciao,
Diana Camelione, Principal

To Diana Camelione, Principal:

Apparently, I have not made it sufficiently clear that I will not be signing anything, not now or in the future, and that I will no longer agree to meet with you unless my union representative is present. I realize that the superintendent is presently negotiating a contract with union leaders that may seriously compromise the rights of teachers. However, I can't imagine such a detrimental contract will be approved by the rank and file membership, of which, in this hour of darkness, I have never been so proud to be a member.

Let this letter serve as official notice that Mrs. Lavinia Sparks will not be going anywhere.

Regarding the cluster of students clamoring for the services of Nurse Fine, perhaps you might consider arranging for her presence more than one day a week. The fifth-grade parents and I eagerly await the District report regarding exactly which substance is responsible for the fumes seeping through the floor of our portable. Until then, we will be taking an extra recess in the morning and an extra recess in the afternoon for the purpose of "airing out" our minds.

Mrs. Sparks
Cc: Superintendent Richard Manheim
        Union President Geoffrey Sterling
        PTA President Gloria Moore

P.S. The girl you noticed "prostrate in the middle of the hall" was Saida Mohammed, who normally uses Nurse Fine's closet to say her prayers. However, since that space is no longer available, due to the surge in students needing medical attention, Miss Mohammed chose a discreet corner in which to say her prayers, far out of anyone's path. We have since found a more suitable space for her and other Muslim students to pray: Coach Birdsong's office.

To Lavinia Sparks, 5th Grade Teacher:

You are not free to negotiate space or anything else involving students at this school. The chain of command is clear. All requests must first come to me. In future, refer any students, parents, or visitors needing direction to the main office where Ms. Macabuhay can triage them. Your services are no longer needed.

Diana Camelione

•

Miz Sparks had been stripped of her power to lead, and now it seemed she might be robbed of her dignity as well. All threats to the contrary, she realized her time had come to leave, just as surely as if her time had come to die. First a fierce struggle, followed by a lovely calm. Slowly she would come to accept the unacceptable truth of her life, that for all the lives she may have saved, she had been helpless to save the one that meant the most—the life of her only child.

She didn't know whom to pray to about her current predicament. The Lord had other people to worry about and He didn't like schoolhouse politics any more than the other gods did. Zeus hadn't sent the promised bolts of lightening to smite the new principal. Athena had proffered neither strength nor wisdom. Perseus was busy elsewhere. Only Pandora showed up in a pinch, and she was no use at all. So Lavinia prayed to the Angel Nathaniel to intercede on her behalf. In a whisper, she dared to utter his name.

Nathaniel. Gift of God. Is it time to give up? Show me a sign. And on this evening of her strange and vast humiliation, He sent a messenger to her door.

It took awhile to recognize her original infantryman.

"Giovanni, is that you? What brings you here tonight? Come on in. I'll fix you some tea."

"Thank you kindly, Miz Sparks. I didn't know if you still lived here. My mama said to tell you hi."

He stooped down and kissed her on the cheek.

"How is your mother? And your sister? I haven't seen y'all in ages."

"We moved back to Italy."

"Where in Italy?"

"Turin. Where my mama's from. I'm here on a business trip."

In his left hand, he carried a misshapen Manila envelope.

"Well you sure look fine. Have you got a family of your own now?"

"Not yet," he laughed. "I'm too young to get married."

"You're more than thirty years old. How old do you have to be?"

"I guess you can say I'm not ready." He looked at his black leather boots. He had always been a stylish young man.

She went to the kitchen and put on the kettle. He followed behind her, took a seat at the table. "Wow. When I think of all the meals we had around this table . . . Those corn pancakes Nate and I used to make. Do you remember? Batter everywhere."

"I try to forget."

"Yeah." He took a deep breath. "I saw Carlos the other day. He told me about Mr. Sparks. I came to offer my condolences."

"Thank you, Giovanni. I remember when you lost your father."

"I was in your class, wasn't I? I gave you a hard time."

"You did."

"Do you forgive me?"

"Do you need to be forgiven?" His brown cheeks went terra cotta. He turned away.

"Tell me why you came, Giovanni."

He stared out the kitchen window. She turned off the kettle and waited for him to stop steaming.

"It's about Nathaniel, isn't it?"

"Yes. These are some letters he wrote when we were kids. I thought you might like to have them." He handed her the envelope.

"Don't you want to keep them?"

"I can hear his voice when I read them."

"You loved him."

"Yes. I loved Nathaniel with all my heart."

He looked her dead in the eyes.

"But not as much as he loved you?"

"No, Ma'am. Not in the same way."

"You keep his letters, Giovanni. I don't want to read them. I can't bear to."

He rubbed his palms on his jeans.

"I don't think he took his life, Ma'am. We'd been drinking. I think he slipped and couldn't lift himself out of the water."

"Is that what you think?"

"Yes, Miz Sparks, that's what I think."

"You're a good boy, Giovanni. You'll make someone very happy someday. But I don't want your letters. Nathaniel wanted you to have them. You keep them. There's nothing to forgive."

He grabbed the envelope and raised his long body from the chair. Before he departed, he leaned down to kiss her on the cheek.

"If I have a son, I'm going to name him Nathaniel," he whispered in her ear.

For a long time, she sat by herself at the kitchen table. Hopes and memories passed each other in the fading light. There was no way to make things right again. How could she have misread all the warning signs? What persistent blindness caused her to ignore what was obvious to others? The sun had long left the sky when she finally went to bed.

Principal Camelione: Occupational Hazards

My door is always open
Please bow before you close the door
I appreciate your feedback
Please bow before you close the door
I'm always open to suggestion
Please bow before you close the door
I take suggestions very seriously
Please bow before you close the door
I pride myself on being approachable
Please bow before you close the door
Don't hesitate to call on me
Please bow before you close the door
My door is always open

There are rules, protocols,
procedures, handbooks, forms,
lots of forms, steps, standards,
rubrics, spreadsheets, guidelines,
regulations, certifications, contracts,
degrees, measures, indices, licenses,
evaluations, re-evaluations,
re-re-evaluations,
ministrations from
administrations with
mission statements and
authorizations to
hold deportations
for insubordinates whose
insubordinations resist
the proper channels, which
are not available at the moment.

This is a restricted area.
Sensitive information is being discussed.
Students are not allowed beyond this point.
Big people are making decisions behind closed doors.
Children who venture into these parts may be
chased away or eaten by the likes of:
La Llorona
The Bogeyman
Humpty Dumpty
Mr. McGregor
Three Blind Mice
The Baby Who Rocked the Tree Top
The Wolf Who Salivated Over Red Riding Hood
The Witch Who Fattened Up Hansel and Gretel
And a host of other scary characters
Who have plans to steal your future.

I do not discriminate on the basis of race, color, age, religion,
national origin, sex, sexual orientation, IQ, disability, looks,
height, weight, number of children.
I am an equal-opportunity employer.
I am equally evil to everyone.
Translation services are available.

阻拦 [zŭlán]

لوخدلا مدع

안에 들이지 않다, 밖에 있다

Your future is in my hands.
If you play by my rules, we'll get along fine.
If you're not with me, you're against me.
I don't care what you did before.
You serve at my discretion.
Pests must be eliminated.
Enter at your own risk.

I drilled down to the facts
by synthesizing data streams
and synergizing measurable outcomes
of tangible goals from replicable models
leading to a paradigm shift involving revisioning
at the same time giving a heads up to our clientele by
messaging the necessity of interfacing with mentor texts
contextualizing our terminal objectives by analyzing factors
that expound on our preliminary evaluations and assessments
vis-à-vis et cetera in exegis ipso facto ad nauseum
in loco parentis ad infinitum caveat emptor
annus horribilis reductio ad absurdum
pursuant to my derrière extremus.
Does anyone have a wonder?
Oops, quick inquiry.
Let's upfront that.
Then, let's move on to
the second item on our agenda:
Optimizing the Decoding of Cognates

Raw Score (RS): 107
Percent Correct (PC): 39
Grade Equivalent (GE): 3.2
Standard Score (SS): 183
Percentile Rank (PR): 16
According to our:
Algorithms
Metrics
Clusters
Vectors
Your child is a failure.
He reads at the ninth-grade level.
He speaks like an English professor.
He plays the violin and the cello.
He holds two patents in physics.
Have you considered a tutor?

At my last school they loved me.
At my last school they honored me.
They gave a huge party in my name.
When they found out I was leaving,
They could scarcely hide their grieving.
Their meager lives would never be the same.
The people here are different,
Not fond of new approaches.
But progress is relentless.
The marketplace encroaches.
To impose higher standards
From reform-based ganders
Pushing fresh pedagogies
On recalcitrant stodgies.
I'm an education warrior.
I get along with everyone,
Especially my immediate superior.

Students have reported:
Swelling and discoloration,
Weakness and dizziness,
Nausea and vomiting,
Sweating and chills,
Pain and tingling.
Children are highly susceptible,
Children are highly suggestible.
I've asked the custodian to investigate.
These are strange, suspicious symptoms.
I've demanded the nurse investigate.
We need the kids to be in tip top shape.
We don't want this thing to spread.
It's almost time to take the Test.
Anyone trying to avoid work
Will answer directly to me.
My bite is worse than my bark.

Use Extreme Caution
roads are slick
trees fallen
black ice
whiteout conditions
wind gusts up to 60 mph
debris blocking the roadway
rivers overflowing their banks
cars abandoned along the highway
accidents involving several vehicles
avalanche warnings in the mountains
semis overturned on the interstate
torrential rains mixed with snow
fires resulting from gas leaks
fog limiting visibility
watch for mudslides
power lines down
road rage

Nurse Fine: First, Do No Harm

Winter comes and comfort goes
Winter comes and comfort goes
Now every time I check my door,
Children cry and sing their woes

The first rule is to do no harm
The first rule is to do no harm
They claim their little heads are hurting
And now I'm sounding the alarm

Heads and shoulders, knees and toes
Heads and shoulders, knees and toes
Oh, my eyes are mighty sore
To say nothing of my ears, my mouth, and my little nose

Well, it's scary raising kids these days
You know, it's scary raising kids these days
Well, it's scary raising kids these days
You know, it's scary raising kids these days
And it's hard to keep them healthy
Inside a riboflavin haze

Junk will make you crazy
And carcinogens abound
Junk will make you crazy
And carcinogens abound
I said it's hard to keep them healthy
With all these chemicals around

Now, cellphones breed suspicion
And those earphones cause a fuss
Cellphones breed suspicion
And those earphones cause a fuss
While in school you need permission
So there's nothing to discuss

Now put away your iPhones
Leave your music at the door
I said put away your iPhones
Leave your music at the door
Don't try to plug your chargers
In the outlets on the floor

Yelling fills the hallways
Screeching voices on the rise
Yelling fills the hallways
Screeching voices on the rise
They echo off the walls and ceilings
Eardrums reeling from the noise

Chatter clogs the airwaves
Playground scuffles pierce the skies
Chatter clogs the airwaves
Playground scuffles pierce the skies
Clatter clutters up the lunchroom
Causing Coach to lose his poise

Stripper, sealant, varnish
They ain't meant for prying eyes
Stripper, sealant, varnish
They ain't meant for prying eyes
Keep your grubby little hands off
Them custodian supplies

Bottles of disinfectent
Must stay safely out of reach
Bottles of disinfectent
Must stay safely out of reach
And when teachers are expecting
Don't be bringing out no bleach

Sugar ants and roaches,
Squirrels and rodents, wasps and bees
Sugar ants and roaches,
Squirrels and rodents, wasps and bees
I've watched these pesky creatures
Bring a building to its knees

I've watched them go 'bout spreadin'
Phobic fear and dread disease
I've watched them go 'bout spreadin'
Phobic fear and dread disease
Bedbugs worse than head lice,
Not to mention mites and fleas

Parents warn your youngsters
Lead paint causes sharp delays
Parents warn your youngsters
Lead paint causes sharp delays
So don't be eating lead paint
'less you want to be half-crazed

Parents warn your youngsters
Keep your sons and daughters well
Parents warn your youngsters
Keep your sons and daughters well
Tell them not to drink the water
They got merc'ry in that well

If I were you I'd stick to
Them little ramen noodle bowls
If I were you I'd stick to
Them little ramen noodle bowls
Don't eat the limp burritos
Avoid the breakfast rolls

Best pass up the orange red sauce
If you know what's good for you
Best pass up the orange red sauce
If you know what's good for you
Try the yellow ravioli
Falsche weinerschnitzel too

When I was but a wee girl
I loved the ling'ring smell
The way the smoke rose in a swirl
And the lovely ashes fell

I said I loved the ling'ring smell
How all other odors vanished
The way those lovely ashes fell
And how foul with foul was banished

Yes, all the other odors vanish
When smoke rises in a band
And soon foul with foul is banished
When I light my fav'rite brand

Dr. Goodwin: Danger, Narrow Road

The sky was a meadow of gold above the mulberry tree.
The fields spread like silky white foam upon a shifting sea.
The wind led a rowdy dance the day that you were born.
And all the bells were ringing –
      Ringing, ringing, ringing –
And all the bells were ringing that sacred winter morn.

You were smart as could be, we could easily see by your eyes.
Your bright and lively countenance held the counsel of the wise.
Nurses who came to meet you were startled by your look.
Your tiny fingers were clinging –
      Clasping, grasping, clinging –
Your tiny fingers were clinging to the pages of a book.

Your father and I started planning where you would go to school.
We opened a college savings account as soon as you could drool.
Above your crib we placed the periodic table.
At night we sang sweet lullabies –
                Jazzing, swinging, singing –
And we taught you how to harmonize as soon as you were able.

But most people only noticed the curls inside your hair.
They admired its wooly texture, its need for loving care.
They bade us tie a ribbon round your soft little baby head.
Bind a pink band of worry –
                Binding, winding, blinding –
Slinging a pink band of worry round your sweet little baby head.

When it came time for preschool, you could already count by five,
Recite doubles to one hundred, find hexagons in a hive,
Play octaves on a piano, make circles out of string,
And you had memorized the names –
         Animal, botanical, tyrranical –
Why, you had memorized the names of every living thing.

We approached the Ivy League Preschool, but they wanted 30 grand.
La Petite Retraite favored kids born in foreign lands.
Musical Prodigy Square couldn't have been any duller.
For all the places we visited –
         Ten, eleven, twelve
We saw only one, two, maybe, three precious kids of color.

I asked around the neighborhood and found a lovely woman
Who had a preschool in her house with hat boxes for drummin'.
Her laugh was such a winsome thing, I instantly adored her.
She took the children caroling –
        Barreling through the snow—
And best of all, as I recall, our budget could afford her.

At graduation you sang an aria in Italian,
Draped around your neck, a lotus blossom medallion.
The other kids all loved you; your patience was impressive.
Your teacher thought you resplendent –
        Creative, independent –
She'd never quite met anyone so naturally expressive.

Kindergarten seemed like a fine time for flirtation
With a Montessori classroom in its local permutation.
But the kids were antisocial, and the parents were conceited,
And the teachers were standoffish –
         Self-actualization, repeated –
At the end of every day, you were thoroughly depleted.

So halfway through the year, we tried a Catholic education,
But soon we were entangled in a thorny situation.
The principal was fired, and the pastor was retired.
The teacher took a leave of absence –
         Abstinence, past tense –
And before long we were paying for a lease, newly acquired.

After extricating faith from the failings of the faithful,
We went on to pledge allegiance to the new and ever grateful
Leaders who took over and attempted to move forward
With a prayer for our salvation –
            If you dare, renunciation –
Too bad tuition's nonrefundable. Christian soldiers, onward.

By now, my child, you were confused as to why you needed school.
Your experience exposed it as an insufficient tool.
You could learn more in a garden. (Did garten have a meaning?)
By exploring your environment –
            Dirt, sand, nix the cement –
We hoped to find a kinder kind than kindergardemeaning.

Let's give the public school a turn; our neighbors like it fine.
It's not a building soon to close; and that's a hopeful sign.
The preschool friends who go there seem like mighty happy clams.
Felicity, you're sure to thrive—
        Socially, for certain –
You're all prepared to take your place among those little lambs.

Who knew they had a waiting list? Now what are we to do?
The nearby charter school is run by military crew.
Home schooling's not an option; our careers would truly suffer.
We'll see what else the District offers –
        Worst case, a farther place –
Actually, not so far, but in a neighborhood far tougher.

I grew up in that neighborhood, attended the local school.
I remember when the graffiti came; gang bangers tried to rule.
But the teachers were fantastic, and discipline was heavy.
I managed to learn a thing or two –
        Hasn't changed much, just smaller –
The building is now dilapidated; the District is seeking a levy.

Needless to say, they have a place or two or three or seven.
When the teacher meets Felicity she dies and goes to heaven.
This little girl needs to skip a grade, the principal declares.
But the teacher vows to keep her –
        I need all the scholars I can get –
If you take away this one, I really will succumb, she glares.

The girls are friendly and adorable, wide-eyed and aware.
There's Kiana, Elizabeth, Leilani, Cynthina, Isi, and Claire.
The boys are little gentlemen, Algernon, Tuan, and Marcus.
There's one girl in the corner –
                A boy sobbing under a table –
But other than that, all seems intact, no noticeable fracas.

First grade passes without incident, much to our relief.
You learn to speak some Spanish, to create a coral reef.
There's only one kid you don't like; you say she is a bully.
But school is an exciting place –
                Hands-on, warm, engaging –
And for the first time since preschool, you'r mind is working fully.

In second grade, your teacher knits, skates, quilts, and cooks.
You learn to write and illustrate your own bright chapter books.
The class is getting bigger, but the kids don't misbehave.
For all intents and purposes –
                    Learning takes place –
You advance your worldly knowledge of what it means to be brave.

Courage comes in handy when your father finds a thrill
Spending the next year working in Brazil.
With a plastic surgeon friend, cleft palates I do mend
And fix the bites of scores of kids –
                    Brave like you, only on the skids –
While your father soothes the tender joints that ache and throb
    and bend.

When we come back to the States, your Portuguese is first rate.
You know how to *samba no pé* but have forgotten how to susurrate.
Your capoeira skills are the envy of your cousins.
You can jump and kick so high –
   She can practically fly! –
And those fancy futebal drills, you can run them by the dozens.

We want you to go to private school, but you won't even hear it.
You'll return to your old school, we agree, although we surely fear it.
When you spend a year of life abroad, nothing ever is the same.
Parting makes for sweet sorrows –
   It confounds our tomorrows –
But nothing compares to returning home wearing a foreign name.

Most of the kids were glad to see you, or surely they pretended.
Since you'd been gone, many friendships were upended.
Remember the girl in the corner? Antipathy Brown?
Can you believe that clown? –
        Now she runs the whole town! –
Be careful when you walk by her. You could end up face down.

A kid named Pedro has no friends, so you sit next to him.
The teacher trusts you to act right; she seems a wee bit dim.
A first-year teacher, she's naive, too timid for this ride.
Why did we two let you decide –
        To retrace your steps –
Instead of stepping from the past to grasp the other side?

The school has a new principal now; her name is Camelione.
When she comes to greet the parents, I catch a whiff of phony.
She says she's all about the numbers, test scores and the like.
What about the children? –
                 This from a grandma –
The kids will have to try harder for their scores to spike.

Plenty of rumbling in that room; the new boss hasn't got a clue.
Who does she think she is coming up here telling us what to do?
Speaking of numbers, hers are quite low, according to the stats.
She's moved from school to school –
                 One of the ones nobody wants –
Drats! Why does the District conspire to send us the dingbats?

You do your part, my daughter, to bring up the test average.
Fourth grade is dull; an old new kid doesn't have much leverage.
Goodwin and I cheer from the side whenever you score a goal.
And all the while we marvel –
    No little girl anymore –
Your determination to grow reveals your wise old soul.

You want to stay for fifth grade and graduate with your class.
We'll find a private middle school, wait for the year to pass.
You've made a friend named Xochitl, another exceptional child.
Fifth grade is bound to be better –
    At least, you'll have Miz Sparks –
She was my teacher three decades ago; she's still plenty wild.

Alas, not even Miz Sparks can make sense of these proceedings.
She's forbidden to give you kids the proper care and feedings.
No Shakespeare this year, not if she wants to keep her position.
Where would I be without her? –
        Desdemona, Ophelia, Juliet –
Lady Macbeth and Beatrice opened a world of ambition.

I joined the parent group, but they acted kind of crazy.
When I couldn't make every meeting, they told me I was lazy.
I sent Goodwin to check them out; he came home with a migraine.
Way too much commotion –
        Shouting, pouting, storming out –
The minutes were offensive; the budget gave him eyestrain.

But he kept going back again, extra helpings for good measure.
He thought it was important to register his displeasure.
While visiting other classrooms, he noted a lack of concentration,
A dearth of reflective activities –
           Music, drawing, gardening –
Things that require self-discipline and encourage observation.

Perhaps we could raise money for an after-school arts camp.
Perhaps we could raise money to purchase a postage stamp.
Perhaps we could hire buses for a field trip to the moon.
Do we look like a private school to you? –
           Perhaps you could be our treasurer –
Field trips, arts camps, postage stamps, September until June.

We've got to get out of here, baby, before we lose our minds.
Your daddy and I have never been the overly litigious kinds.
This school is driving us crazy; there's something in the air.
You're fighting in class –
            Impossible, regrettable –
You must have been driven to madness by a system truly unfair.

You said you were being bullied, that you weren't the only one.
We talked with Miz Sparks about it; she clearly was outdone.
She spoke to Minor and to Camelione, too. They accused her.
Classroom management, it's your job –
            To control that Brown kid –
You know, we're in the ghetto, kids on crack, they excused her.

They say that education is the civil rights cause of our day.
If I thought conspiracies real, I'd say it was planned that way.
At the time of integration, that's when the barriers got raised.
Brown children aren't supposed to excel –
              No poll tax, no math facts, no rules –
Let's just hand the whole place over to the certifiably crazed.

I'm sorry you suffered, my daughter, sorry you lost your zeal.
It's time for you to go where you won't have to wheel and deal.
We may need to borrow some money from your university share.
At least we got to save some –
              You got some and you gave some—
Now you're aware life is unfair. It's time to straighten your hair.

Coach Birdsong: School Zone, 20 MPH

If life were fair, each child would find
A stable parent, strong and kind
The kind of person capable
Of burdens inescapable
The kind of love, the kind of joy
That far outweigh the grandest toy
The kindest heart in finest shape
Around which tiny arms can drape
Not parents who from duties run
In search of endless rounds of fun
Whose cars are where their passions lie
Who spend their weekends getting high
Who haven't grace nor strength of mind
To bring up children, strong and kind

The road is long, the path is steep
For children who are born asleep
In sleep they try to find their way
Through longest night and darkest day
In sleep they hum a lonely hymn
When no one comes to comfort them
In sleep they wish to always be
For wake their lives bleed misery
And all their dreams are marred by pain
And all their hopes flow down the drain
If only they could throw away
The garbage that their parents say
It's hard to rise above the heap
When born to parents dead asleep

To narrow spacious "budget gaps"
The District institutes "no caps"
No caps on classroom size or range
Just padlocks on all pocket change
No caps on large consultants' fees
Just lids on teachers' salaries
No caps on bonuses for crooks
Just bans on controversial books
No baseball caps, no colored rags,
No gansta raps, no khaki sags,
No tattoos, logos, signs, or tags,
No forties, 8-balls, nickel bags,
To tackle our "achievement gaps"
The District institutes "no caps"

Be careful, or you're bound to meet
The sex offender down the street
The street our children walk to school
Where gangs await and hoodlums rule
The street wherein his mother lives
Whose Christian faith all sins forgives
The street he walked to school each morn
Before this generation born
Inside these walls he did his math
And shook these halls with fits of wrath
He stood outside the bathroom doors
And taunted kids who peed on floors
Beware the urge to blithely greet
The sex offender down the street

I've seen more people ruined by
The demon drink than any high
Than any vice—from coke to crack
From rolls of weed to bags of smack
Than any higher power trip
That ends in Kool-Aid or Cool Whip
Than any mushrooms in the wild
Or even love unreconciled
First one sip take and then another
Slick offer from an older brother
And soon you're in a fathom deep
The juice so good it makes you weep
Then quick to sneak and steal and lie
The demon drink is ever nigh

As far as trying drugs may go
Quick, turn your back and just say no
Say no to huffing model glue
Or disinfectant residue
Say no to grandpa's painkillers
And grandma's mindless brain thrillers
Say no to all the star athletes
who don't succeed by downing sweets
and lawyers with their mounds of coke
who leave their desks to take a toke
and doctors dealing drugs to make
their portion of the druggists' take
Success comes down to making dough
So cross your heart and just say no

The leading risk for weapons crime
is parent-teacher conference time
A time when children ill-behaved
Show off their families, most depraved
A time when fathers seldom seen
Show up for teachers' clocks to clean
A time when manic mothers stalk
And deck the halls with threatening talk
And teachers young and teachers old
Try not to speak in terms too bold
Please check your weapons at the door
And keep your steel toes on the floor
Lest teachers start to pistols buy
At parent-teacher conference time

Drown all your flames in tepid streams
Awake no storms, advance no dreams
Ban all ideas involving dance
Arouse no passion, take no chance
Shelve thoughts expressed in paint and clay
Shoo all that messy art away
Mute tales told loudly from the stage
Bar captured fury from the page
No testimonies marked by tears
No zany aunts, no flaming queers
Spontaneous combustion might
Set all the children's pain alight
And what will all the bosses say
If hearts ignite and claim the day

NO
LOITERING
ON THIS
PROPERTY

You're here to work, not fool around
School needs to be your solid ground
The solid ground beneath your feet
When chaos occupies the street
The fertile ground in which to plant
When nutrients at home are scant
The hallowed ground in faith decreed
By ancestors who couldn't read
Learn all you may from all who know
A portion of what makes things so
Learn how to be the best you can
Pursue your freedom, make your plan
We all know school can be plain hard
But playgrounds beat the prison yard

Antipathy Brown: Run, Storm

Psalm 71: 1-4
¹ In you, O Lord, I take refuge;
let me never be put to shame.
² In your righteousness deliver me.
Incline your ear to me and save me.
³ Be to me a rock of refuge,
to which I may always come;
you have given the command to save me,
for you are my rock and my fortress.
⁴ Rescue me, O God, from the hand of the wicked,
from the grasp of the unjust man.

My mother told me to shake his hand, but I didn't want to shake his hand. He's your uncle she said, shake his hand. But if he was my uncle, how come I didn't know him? He's daddy's half-brother, she said. I said he's nothing to me, and I didn't shake his hand. Why do I have to sleep on the couch? He can sleep on the couch.

The place where we stay is a basement. It has two skinny beds and a couch and a table. When it rains hard, the water comes through the cracks in the floor. My mother says God is here, even when it's cold and damp. God is everywhere. He sees everything.

> *After the storm there's a rainbow.*
> *God carry me through this storm.*
> *Every cloud has a silver lining.*
> *God speak to me in the thunder.*
> *God never closes a door without opening a window.*

Psalm 57: 4
My soul is lost among lions;
I lie down amid fiery beasts –
the children of man,
whose teeth are spears and arrows,
whose tongues are sharp swords.

Every Saturday night my father's friends come over to play cards and drink. Why can't I have friends over, I say? We could play cards and drink soda. But the basement stinks like smoke and drink, so none of my friends, if I really had friends, would want to come over anyway.

Pedro is my friend. He let me come over to his house one day. He's like my little brother. I take care of him, and he brings me lunch. We were eating popcorn when his foster mother came home, and she was really mad because we burned the popcorn, and we were sitting there eating burnt popcorn and watching TV. The next day at school we laughed about it. Pedro always laughs at my jokes. That's why he's my friend. He doesn't call me names either. Sometimes I call him names though. When he makes me mad.

My daddy's friends call him names and rag on him. Then they get drunk and fall asleep. I bury my head in my pillow, so I don't have to smell their stink. We only have one tiny bathroom, and sometimes my mother has to get up and bleach it in the middle of the night. My father's friends complain about the bleach, but at least it makes them get up and leave.

> *God let the lion lay down with the lamb.*
> *God protect me from the lion.*
> *The lions ate the Christians but they didn't eat Daniel.*
> *Jesus called the little children unto Him.*

Psalm 58: 6-7
⁶ O God, break the teeth in their mouths;
tear out the fangs of the young lions.
⁷ Let them vanish like water that runs away;
when they aim their arrows, let them fall short.

One night I was sleeping and they started shooting outside. A bullet came through the basement window and landed in the sink. I was screaming like it was thunder and lightning. My mother put her arms around me and told me to be quiet because they might still be out there.

One time there was this gang fight and they arrested my cousin. It was his third strike. He was on the news. They showed him from behind. He had chains on his hands and on his feet too.

Lightning never strikes twice.
Three strikes and you're out.
The voice of the Lord strikes with flashes of lightning.
I hear Him in the thunder.

He smites the unbeliever.
Satan fell like lightning from Heaven.
God will strike his enemies dead.
God will strike my enemies dead too.

Psalm 59: 14-15
¹⁴ Each evening they come back,
howling like dogs,
prowling about the city.
¹⁵ They wander looking for food,
growl if they do not find it.

One day I brought this dog home and my mother said I could keep her as long as she stayed in the yard. Her name is Paradise. I asked my mother what kind of dog she is, and she said a street dog. She's kind of ugly but she's smart. I let her come inside when nobody's home, then quick send her out before they come through the door. My mother got mad because she found a flea, so I had to give Paradise a bath.

Paradise likes to run like hell all over the house.

Paradise attacked one of my father's friends and sent him to the hospital. He tried to fight her off by barking and growling, but she charged him and chased him around the yard. She caught him trying to sneak in the back way one evening. My father said that's what he gets for trying to sneak in the back way. She didn't let him go till my mother beat her off with a stick.

After that since we both were feeling injured, Paradise got to sleep on the couch with me. She tries to protect me. It's 'cause I took her in. Whenever I have something to eat, I give her a little corner.

They say dogs can't eat chocolate, but Paradise will eat anything. I think she could eat a whole man, if she wanted to.

God deliver me from evildoers and save me from those
who are after my blood.

Psalm 5.4
Tremble and do not sin;
when you are on your beds,
search your hearts and be silent.

I don't want to do the homework my teacher sent, so my mother makes me read the Bible instead. Everyday I read one of the Psalms. I just open the Bible to any page that has a Psalm, and then I read it and try to memorize some of it so I can tell my mother when she comes home.

My mother works odd jobs. Some days she helps run the food bank, and then she gets to pick out something special to bring me. One day this lady dropped off seventeen jars of peaches and my mother brought one home. I ate peaches for a whole week. I didn't give Paradise any.

This man knocked on the door and said he knew we were hiding my uncle who's not really my uncle because he owed him some money. My mother told him to go away or she would call the police. Paradise was barking like crazy. I said, Get him Paradise. He wouldn't stop pounding on the door.

Finally he kicked in the door and grabbed the microwave off the table. He had a gun. He said he was going to shoot Paradise if she didn't stop barking. He told mommy to give him all her money. She said she didn't have no money, so he took her ring instead. That same day, she kicked my uncle out.

> *Stop thief.*
> *Stop before I shoot.*
> *Stop looking at me.*
> *Stop before I hit you.*
> *God will stop you in your tracks.*
> *Stop or I'll tell somebody.*

Psalm 3:7
Arise, O Lord. Save me, O God.
You strike my enemies on the cheek;
you break the teeth of the wicked.

It's been almost a week since they let me come to school. My mother said they have to go to a meeting to get me back in. They said I had too many suspensions to go back. That's because people make me mad, and they never do anything about it.

One day I broke down in front of the teacher because I was hungry. Pedro was sick and the school lunch is never enough, so I was mad because I was hungry. She kept asking me questions about my home life, and I told her it wasn't her business, and then I called her a name. She always tries to get in my business.

Don't let hunger happen to you.
Let justice roll down like water.
Let there be peace on earth.
Don't leave home without it.

Psalm 112:10
The wicked man sees and is angry;
he gnashes his teeth and melts away;
the desire of the wicked will perish.

The neighbors upstairs are drug dealers, so I have to stay out of their way. If you get into other people's business, you can get hurt. One time some people busted in and took all their money but nobody got hurt. Sometimes my mother does odd jobs for them.

Don't tell anybody what goes on in this house. It's none of their business. If you tell our business they'll take you away. You don't want to be taken away, do you? If they take you away, they won't let you keep Paradise. You don't want to live with strangers. Remember, blood is thicker than water.

Everybody talking bout Heav'n ain't goin' there. God, deliver me from evil. If you tell anybody, I'll kill you. Give us this day our daily bread. Here, I bought you some cherries. His eye is on the sparrow and I know He watches me. Have you ever tasted tequila? Forgive us our trespasses, as we forgive those who trespass against us. Let's see if the dog will drink some.

> *God I trust you for protection.*
> *Save me and rescue me from those who are chasing me.*
> *Like a lion they will tear me apart.*
> *They will rip me to pieces and no one can save me.*
> *Lord, what have I done?*
> *Have my hands done something wrong?*

Psalm 22:1-2
¹ My God, my God, why have you forsaken me?
Why are you so far from saving me,
from the words of my groaning?
² O God, I cry by day, but you do not answer,
and by night, I find no rest.

Sometimes I think nobody likes me. Not even Paradise. Sometimes when I try to play with her she growls and tries to bite me. This girl at school kicked me and I got in trouble. My side hurts. My stomach hurts. My shoulder hurts. My eyeballs hurt. All my insides are messed up. It hurts to breathe. My feelings hurt real bad. Mostly I just feel tired of everything. I want all this pain to go away and leave me alone.

Daddy says it takes a long time to heal from some wounds. He's still trying to heal from his foot that got crushed in the war. That's why he hardly ever goes anywhere because it hurts him to walk and he's too proud to use his cane. He says if people see your weakness they will target you.

He tells me to stop crying like a girl. I know he wanted a boy. Most of his friends have lots of kids but he only has me. They like to brag about how many kids they have but it's not like they see them. They're too busy playing cards and drinking. They say, Patmos you ain't much of a man because you only got one kid. He says, he's not sure I'm his because I cry so much, and they all laugh. My mother doesn't think it's funny. She says I'm his all right, or she wouldn't be supporting his crushed foot and sorry ass. That makes them laugh real hard.

O Lord, see how my enemies persecute me.
Have mercy and lift me up from the gates of death.

Psalm 6:6
I am weary with my moaning;
every night I flood my bed with tears;
I drench my couch with my weeping.

I fought when they came to take me away. They were all up in my business. I was too weak to fend them off.

God never gives you more than you can handle. Were you there when they crucified my Lord? Who do you think you are? I am somebody. Jesus is my Savior.

I'm here to help and protect you. Can you understand what I'm saying? I need to touch you in order to find out what's wrong. Try to breathe normally. You may feel some pain and discomfort. You're going to be all right.

Now I lay me down to sleep.
I pray the Lord my soul to keep.
May God guard me throughout the night.
And wake me with the morning light.
But if I die before I wake I pray to God my soul to take.

14 / All in Favor

First Order of Business:
Mrs. Gloria Moore: For those of you who don't know me, I am Gloria Moore, Kiana's mother, and the Muhammad Ali Elementary School PTA President. Welcome to the Emergency Mandatory Meeting for the Fifth Grade Parents of Miz Sparks's Class. Please introduce yourself and spell your name, so Mrs. Queenie Johnson can put you in the minutes.

Officers in Attendance:
Gloria Moore, President (Kiana)
Stephanie Anderson, Vice President (3rd-grade parent)
Dennis Takahashi, Co-Vice President (Kenji)
Queenie Johnson, Secretary (Princess)

School Staff in Attendance:
Miz Lavinia Sparks, 5th-Grade Teacher
Nurse Sharon Fine, Nurse
Miss Juanita Macabuhay, Secretary
Major Jake Minor, Vice Principal
Mister Curtis Birdsong, Coach

People Notably Absent:
Mr. Tracy Goodwin, Treasurer (Felicity)
Mrs. Diana Camelione, Principal
The Allens (Has anybody ever seen them?)

Special Guest Speaker Parents:
Mrs. Antigone Brown (Antipathy)
Mr. Patmos Brown (Ditto)
Dr. Sylvia Goodwin (See Tracy)

Other People in Attendance:
 African Americans
All the Officers (except Takahashi)
All the Guest Speakers

Miss Eleanor Thompson (Marcus)
Mr. Joseph Metoyer (Algernon, they don't look black but they are)
Ms. Sophie Davis and Mr. Clyde Walker (Claire)
Grandma Ida (De'Andre Jackson)
Miss Arnetta White (foster grandmother of Pedro Brayboy)
Mrs. Coriander Jones, Jr. (Zachary, III)
Mr. Ray Lewis (Will Robinson, Jr.)
Miss Dorothy Young (Quincy Smith)
> *Asians*
Mr. and Mrs. Nguyen (Tuan, Lien)
Mr. Hoang Pham and Mrs. Khanh Lam (Bao, Khanh, Vinh)
Mr. Vu Truong, Vietnamese Interpreter
Mrs. Frances Yang (Elizabeth, not Vietnamese, doesn't need interpreter)
Mr. Choi (don't know who his kid is)
> *Hispanics*
Mr. Jesus and Mrs. Maria Rivera (Efraím, Laura, and the baby)
Mr. Angel Hernandez (Xochitl)
Mrs. Teresa Martinez (Omar, Angelito)
Mr. Diego Martinez (Didn't he have a restraining order?)
A bunch of cousins, aunts, and uncles
> *White People*
Ms. Lucinda Wilson (Is she white?) and Mr. Evan Clarke (Harry)
Ms. Constance Miller and Ms. Prudence Resnik (Netanya and Netanya)
> *Other Others*
Mrs. Vanessa Edwards (Isi, Fala, Nita, Choctaw)
Mr. Fetu Lemalu (Lea and Aleki, Samoan)
Mrs. Louise Balthazar (Renard, claims to be Cajun)
Mr. David Ladu (Elijah, from the Congo)
Mr. Tadesse Teklemariam (Jerusalem, Ethiopian)
Mr. Dev Patel (Jayan, Indian)
All the Mohammeds (Saida, Somali)
Mrs. Athena Kruse (Serena, Lebanese)
Mrs. Catalina Dumlao (Genevieve, Filipino)

Call to Order:

Mrs. Gloria Moore: I call to order this mandatory emergency meeting of the PTA in special session to deal with students getting sick and other problems in Miz Sparks's class. Will all the students that are here please stand up? Let's thank the students for coming, even though they may not feel well. Okay, kids, you can sit down. Now, Mrs. Queenie Johnson, yours truly, will submit the minutes from our last meeting, which was secret, so there are no minutes. Can I get a motion?.

A motion was made and seconded.

The motion was carried.

The minutes were approved.

Old Business:

A motion was made to suspend old business so we could get down to new business, which is the reason that we're here because all these children are getting sick from unknown causes.

A vote was called for and taken.

All in favor.

New Business:

Mrs. Gloria Moore: What's going on in Miz Sparks's room?

A hand was raised and recognized.

Princess: It's been crazy up in there. Everybody been fallin' out like they was in church. Their eyes be rollin' back in they heads and . . .

(The speaker got carried away. A new speaker was given the floor.)

Marcus: Some people are faking it.

De'Andre: How do you know?

Grandma Ida: De'Andre, sit down. Raise your hand.

Claire: How can you say people are faking it? What evidence do you have?

Jayan: People thought I was faking it, and I ended up in the emergency room.

Mrs. Gloria Moore: Please raise your hand if you wish to speak.

Mr. Patmos Brown: That's right. Speak up, son.

Jayan: How can you tell if you have emphysema?

Nurse Fine: There's a sharp pain in your lungs.

Jayan: How do you know it's not your appendix?

Nurse Fine: Your lungs are in your chest. Your appendix is located in your lower-right abdominal cavity.

Dr. Sylvia Goodwin: Can we please stick to the issue at hand?

Jayan: But what if your appendix is in the wrong place?

Nurse Fine: I've never heard of that happening.

Jayan: I read about a man whose arm was where his nose was supposed to be.

Kenji: That's not possible. How could he breathe?

Serena: Through his mouth.

Genevieve: Or, maybe, with his ears.

The subject was debated.

A hand was raised and recognized.

Mr. Choi: My son is very sick.

Mrs. Gloria Moore: Who's your son?

Mr. Choi: He goes to another school. Same problem.

Mr. Joseph Metoyer: We're talking about this school, Mister. Ding. You're out of order.

Mr. Choi: My name is not Ding. My name is Choi.

Mr. Joseph Metoyer: All right, Bro. Settle down, settle down.

Mrs. Gloria Moore: Mr. Choi, how did you find out about this meeting?

Mr. Choi: Somebody put a flyer in my mailbox.

Mr. Metoyer: You must live next to somebody. It's cool. I mean, we all in this together, right?

Mr. Choi: I just want to know what's going on.

Mrs. Gloria Moore: Don't we all? Don't we all . . . Let's give Mr. Choi a round of applause. Sometimes, the most important thing in life is just to show up.

Ms. Prudence Resnick: Maybe we could take a count of all the students who have been sick and what their symptoms are.

Mrs. Gloria Moore: Do I have a motion?

Mr. Joseph Metoyer: I move that unless you have a kid at this school, you shouldn't be at this meeting.

Mrs. Gloria Moore: Do we have a second?

Xochitl: Maybe we should hear from Miz Sparks first.

Mrs. Gloria Moore: An excellent idea, Xochitl. Miz Sparks, would you care to comment?

Miz Lavinia Sparks: Thank you. I'll try to be brief. I've been keeping a tally of students who reported smelling the odor and having symptoms. In the past three weeks, we've had 9 cases of students feeling dizzy, 23 headaches, 4 heart palpitations, 16 breathing problems, 2 nosebleeds, and 8 cases of nausea.

Mrs. Louise Balthazar: This is the first I'm hearing it. Renard, you got the *faiblesse? Dit mon la verite!*

Renard: Non, Maman. I ain't smell nothin'.

Miss Arnetta White: Is this happening in other classes, too?

Omar: ¿Papi, puedo ir, por favor? Tengo migraña.

Miz Lavinia Sparks: Other classes aren't experiencing the same symptoms because they're located in the main building, which isn't having the same problems. They're having other issues, but I'm not prepared to talk about those at this time.

Mrs. Vanessa Edwards: What kind of issues? Do I have to be worried about my other girls, too?

Miz Lavinia Sparks: I believe their problems have to do with pest control.

De'Andre: They got rats!

Miz Lavinia Sparks: It could be squirrels or some other rodent.

De'Andre: They got big ole rats chasing people down the halls.

Dr. Sylvia Goodwin: Can we please stick to the issue at hand?

Grandma Ida: De', that's enough.

Mr. Fetu Lemalu: Where's the odor coming from?

Miz Lavinia Sparks: The odor seems to be seeping from the ground beneath our portable. Ever since my class was relegated to a portable, I've been having all kinds of symptoms, the most disturbing being the shortness of breath and rapid heartbeats.

(A hand was raised and ignored.)

I complained of these issues many times, but the administration chose to ignore my complaints until recently, when the children started exhibiting the same symptoms I'd been having since October.

(A voice was raised and silenced.)

As you know, many children have been absent due to headaches and dizziness, and Kiana has been out for a whole week trying to control her asthma, which she's never had before.

Mrs. Gloria Moore: Thank you, Miz Sparks. I'm happy to report that Kiana is feeling better, but she's not coming back to school until there's some accountability. At the very least, your classroom needs to be moved to the gym.

An authority figure tried to speak.

The authority figure was roundly denounced.

The authority figure said insulting things.

The authority figure was booed.

The authority figure stated no classes could be held in the gym.

The authority figure was pummeled.

Miss Macabuhay intervened, and the authority figure escaped with his life.

Mrs. Queenie Johnson: Can somebody make a motion?

Ms. Lucinda Wilson: I move that Miz Sparks's classroom be moved to the gym.

Mr. Evan Clarke: I second the motion.

Mrs. Gloria Moore: A motion has been made to move Miz Sparks's classroom to the gym. Is there any discussion? Coach Birdsong, is there a problem?

Coach Curtis Birdsong: We've been having PE outside because of all the debris in the gym, but I think we can get it cleaned up sometime next week. Of course, you might want to check with the principal first. I'm just sayin'...

Mrs. Queenie Johnson: All in favor? It is so moved.

Miss Juanita Macabuhay: The principal asked me to deliver this letter to you, since she could not be here. (The letter was read by Miss Juanita and translated by Nurse Fine.) "To Our Esteemed Customers and Mid-Level Scholars, Ciao."

Nurse Fine: "Dear Fifth-Grade Families, Hello and Goodbye."

Mrs. Gloria Moore: Is that all?

Miss Juanita Macabuhay: No, there's more. "This comes to inform you that I've been queried to extrapolate on academic alignment for a continuum of mastery-focused professionals concerned with implementing open-ended learning structures to power up our Adequate Yearly Progress."

Nurse Fine: "I'm going to schmooze and kvetch with my high-powered friends over cocktails, so I don't have time for you schmucks."

Mr. Dev Patel: It's impossible to understand this woman.

Mrs. Queenie Johnson: Hold up. Y'all are going too fast for me.

Nurse Fine: Just write: "Screw you."

Mrs. Gloria Moore: Let me remind the speaker that there are children present.

Nurse Fine: Your point is well taken. I apologize for my cynicism. The children shouldn't be exposed to this kind of language.

Mrs. Queenie Johnson: Children, cover your ears.

Miss Juanita Macabuhay: May I continue?

Dr. Sylvia Goodwin: Please. Continue. Please.

Miss Juanita Macabuhay: "Scientifically based research can be forwarded to my administrative representative who is trained to track disaggregated data vis-à-vis concurrent processing. Ciao."

Nurse Fine: "If you have something to say, put it in writing and give it to Major Minor, Hello and goodbye to you and you and you too."

Mr. Angel Hernandez: Didn't he leave?

Mrs. Louise Balthazar: Major Minor done skedaddled.

Mr. Fetu Lemalu: He got his butt kicked.

Mrs. Queenie Johnson: Is that all, then?

A topic was introduced and tabled.

An issue was raised and dismissed.

A doubt was voiced and doubted.

An accusation was made and denied.

A compliment was offered and accepted.

Dr. Sylvia Goodwin: Well, I was invited to be a guest speaker, and I really only have one thing to say. I will not continue to send my child to a school where her health is daily compromised.

Mr. Patmos Brown: Amen to that.

Mrs. Gloria Moore: Very well, then. I think we need a plan for moving forward. And whatever steps we decide upon need to have specific names attached to them.

Mr. Ray Lewis: I'd like to volunteer to go talk to the principal. She doesn't like me much, but I think it's important that some parents who are not PTA officers register our disapproval.

Mrs. Gloria Moore: Very good. Do I have other parents who would be willing to accompany Mr. Lewis? Please keep your hands up until Mrs. Queenie Johnson takes down your name.

Mrs. Queenie Johnson: Mr. Lemalu. Thank you. Miss White. Thank you. Mr. Choi, you're not eligible. Will somebody explain to Mr. Choi what's going on? Mr. Brown, I don't think it's a good idea for you to go to this meeting. We don't want to confuse the issues, since you already have business before the principal.

Mrs. Antigone Brown: Sit down, Patmos.

Mr. Patmos Brown: That's right. I'm suing this school for what they've done to my daughter, trying to lower her self-esteem and all.

Mrs. Queenie Johnson: Anyone else? I think it would be good to have a representative from the Hispanic community.

Mr. Angel Hernandez: I'll go.

Mrs. Queenie Johnson: Gracias, Mr. Hernandez. Now, what about you Asians? Can we get an Asian?

Mr. Dennis Takahashi: I'm Asian.

Mrs. Queenie Johnson: Oh, c'mon, Dennis. You know you can't get up in the morning. We need somebody on time.

Mrs. Frances Yang: How long is it going to take?

Mrs. Queenie Johnson: Beats me. As long as it takes.

Mrs. Frances Yang: Forget it, then. I'd rather do jury duty.

Mrs. Queenie Johnson: Really? You can't pay me to do jury duty.

Dr. Sylvia Goodwin: Can we please stick to the issue at hand?

Mrs. Frances Yang: Why don't you ask Mr. Patel? He's Asian.

Mrs. Queenie Johnson: Really? Dev, are you Asian?

Mr. Dev Patel: Indeed. India is a South Asian country.

Mrs. Queenie Johnson: Well, I'll be. You learn something new every day.

Mrs. Gloria Moore: If there's no further discussion, that concludes the new business.

Mr. Patmos Brown: When's it going to be my turn?

Guests Speakers and More New Business:
All hell broke loose when Mr. Patmos Brown, who appeared to be drunk, accused Nurse Fine of being a lesbian who improperly laid her hands on his daughter. Nurse Fine stormed out of the room. It was reported by this writer that Nurse Fine is having an affair with Coach

Birdsong, so she can't be a lesbian. The fact was duly noted. Coach Bird-song declared that his personal life was nobody's business. His wife might beg to differ. He exited the room. Mrs. Gloria Moore asked Mr. Patmos Brown to please sit down.

Decorum was temporarily lost and restored.

Mr. Patel said someone should be responsible for paying his son's hospital bill. Dr. Goodwin agreed, saying she would be willing to help the Patels negotiate with the District. Mr. Patmos Brown said he already had a lawyer and didn't need her help. Dr. Goodwin kindly pointed out that she hadn't offered him any.

Mr. Ray Lewis: Y'all need to stop arguing. It's getting late.

The truth was slowly registered.

All in favor.

The meeting was closed and adjourned.

The chairs were stacked and removed.

15 / Tyrant, Show Thy Face

I couldn't see him. He didn't look like anyone I knew. I couldn't see him. He didn't smell like anyone I knew. I couldn't tell what color he was. I couldn't tell anything about him. I'd never seen him before. He didn't say anything the whole time.

> *Out, damned spot! out, I say! One: two: why,*
> *then, 'tis time to do't. Hell is murky! Fie, my*
> *lord, fie! a soldier, and afeard? What need we*
> *fear who knows it, when none can call our power to*
> *account? Yet who would have thought the old man*
> *to have had so much blood in him.*

He had a knife and he put it up to me. I wasn't really scared 'cause it was a little knife. When I go fishing with Daddy, he lets me gut the fish. I use a big knife to gut the fish.

> *What, will these hands ne'er be clean? No more o'*
> *that, my lord, no more o' that: you mar all with*
> *this starting.*
> *Here's the smell of the blood still: all the*
> *perfumes of Arabia will not sweeten this little*
> *hand. Oh, oh, oh!*
> *Wash your hands, put on your nightgown;*
> *look not so pale. I tell you yet again,*
> *Banquo's buried; he cannot come out on's grave.*
> *To bed, to bed! there's knocking at the gate:*
> *come, come, come, come, give me your hand. What's*
> *done cannot be undone. To bed, to bed, to bed!*

I stabbed him with his knife. That's what I told you the first time and that's what's true. I don't know what happened after that. He was bleeding and he ran away. That's all I know.

Come, you spirits
That tend on mortal thoughts! unsex me here,
And fill me from the crown to the toe, top-full
Of direst cruelty; make thick my blood,
Stop up the access and passage to remorse,
That no compunctious visitings of nature
Shake my fell purpose, nor keep peace between
The effect and it! Come to my woman's breasts,
And take my milk for gall, you murdering ministers,
Wherever in your sightless substances
You wait on nature's mischief!

He touched my breasts and tried to take my pants off. That's when he dropped his knife—he had it between his teeth—and I picked it up and stabbed him in the shoulder. I was scared he was going to stab me back but Paradise bit him good.

I have given suck, and know
How tender 'tis to love the babe that milks me:
I would, while it was smiling in my face,
Have pluck'd my nipple from his boneless gums,
And dash'd the brains out, had I so sworn
As you have done to this.

He wore a mask. How should I know what he looked like? He had on gloves, too. He told me he would kill me if I said a word. That's all I know.

From: "Camelione, Diana" <camelioned@districtschools.org>
To: "Sparks, Lavinia" <sparksl@districtschools.org>
Subject: Inappropriate Use of Language
Date: February 14 11:11 AM

Dear Mrs. Sparks,

I have been very clear in my instructions to abandon the teaching of Shakespeare and concentrate on preparing your students for their standardized tests. The time it took you to stage your play would have been better spent trying to raise our mean test scores.

I needn't tell you how many parents objected to the language in the play nor how unpleasant I personally found the words "unsex me here" falling from the mouth of a fifth-grade girl. Not to mention "plucked my nipple from boneless gums and dashed the brains out." While the teaching of Shakespeare does not rise to the level of an infraction, I feel you are taking every opportunity to fly in the face of my authority.

Furthermore, your attempt to recreate Orson Welles's *Voodoo Macbeth* was deeply offensive to the Christian families in attendance. Finally, I cannot fathom why you would reward a bad actor like Miss Brown with the main role.

In flabbergastedness,
Mrs. Camelione

From: "Sparks, Lavinia" <sparksl@districtschools.org>
To: "Camelione, Diana" <camelioned@districtschools.org>
Subject: Re: Inappropriate Use of Language
Date: February 14 7:35 PM

Dear Mrs. Camelione,

To show an unfelt sorrow is an office which the false (wo)man does easy.

Fair is foul, and foul is fair.
What's done is done.

Ciao,
Lavinia

From: "Camelione, Diana" <camelioned@districtschools.org>
To: "Sparks, Lavinia" <sparksl@districtschools.org>
Subject: Contract for Next School Year
Date: February 14 7:55 PM
Attachments: Memorandum of Understanding (MOU)

Dear Mrs. Sparks,

What's done is you.

This Memorandum of Understanding constitutes your invitation
not to return next year. The District thanks you for your long years of
service and wishes you well in your future endeavors.

Please print and sign the MOU and put it in my mailbox tomorrow
morning.

From: "Sparks, Lavinia" <sparksl@districtschools.org>
To: "Camelione, Diana" <camelioned@districtschools.org>
Cc: "Manheim, Richard" <superintendent@districtschools.org>,
    "Shapiro, Sam" <samstickin2daunion@NTU.org>, "Lau, Pamela"
    <laup@plauassociates>, "Moore, Gloria" <glomo@literacynow
    .org>, "Diop, Josephine" <newstips@C5News.com>
Subject: Misdirected Communications
Date: February 14 8:29 PM
Attachments: Pamela Lau contact information

Principal Camelione,

Please direct all further communications regarding this matter to my
attorney, Pamela Lau, whose contact information is above. Decorum
requires me to notify you that I will not be signing anything. Nor will
I meet with you unless both my union representative and my attorney
are present.

Kindly be advised that I have filed an appeal regarding my most recent evaluation and have a meeting scheduled next week with the Director of Human Resources. Furthermore, I am contesting my untimely dismissal after 32 years of outstanding evaluations under the leadership of 14 different principals.

Sincerely Yours,
Lavinia Sparks

From: "Camelione, Diana" <camelioned@districtschools.org>
To: "Sparks, Lavinia" <sparksl@districtschools.org>
Cc: "Chelsea Clark, Director of Human Resources" <hrd@districtschools.org>
Subject: Contract for Next School Year
Date: February 14 9:03 PM

MS—The Director of Human Resources informed me last week that you had filed an appeal to challenge your most recent evaluation. May I remind you that you refused to sign your evaluation, which means it was submitted under protest. However, this in no way affected my decision to eliminate your position by combining two 4th- and 5th-grade classrooms.

As you are well aware, our school has been losing enrollment for a number of years, due to the fact that the federal No Child Left Behind Act allows parents to transfer their children out of failing schools. Until we get our test scores up, I'm afraid we will continue to lose students and staff. You are not the only one affected by this reality.—DC

From: "Sparks, Lavinia" <sparksl@districtschools.org>
To: "Camelione, Diana" <camelioned@districtschools.org>
Cc: "Johnson, Queenie" <qj2@johnsonconstruction.com>
Subject: Our Shrinking Staff
Date: February 14 9:14 PM

Mrs. Camelione,

I find it disingenuous for you to suggest our staff is shrinking due to lower enrollment when our enrollment has held steady for the last ten years. Numbers of students transferring out have been more than matched by the numbers of students transferring in. And why would parents transfer their children into a failing school? Because they understand that the data is skewed.

The fact that the superintendent plays golf with the CEO of a national charter schools organization has been lost on no one. As the neighborhood undergoes a predictable pattern of gentrification, the District's attempt to shutter Muhammad Ali Elementary School is sadly reminiscent of the kind of tricks employed in the aftermath of *Brown v. The Board of Ed.*

Beginning with the name change designed to erase our history, your mean-spirited campaigns are destined to fail. Your plot to replace me (with some unsuspecting kid from Teach for America) is evidence that you care nothing for the education of our children. And the District's plan to invite a certain ex-chancellor from D.C. to ransack what's left of our teachers' dignity is wholly transparent. Union busting, pure and simple.

I intend to stay on until our grand experiment in universal education has been restored to its original intent: to form a people united by the knowledge necessary to sustain a healthy democracy. Language, literature, history, geography, civics, philosophy, mathematics, science, health, economics, journalism, chess, athletics, the law and the arts—this is what the children are owed. They may not be much, but the public schools are all we have left.

Mrs. Sparks

From: "Camelione, Diana" <camelioned@districtschools.org>
To: "Sparks, Lavinia" <sparksl@districtschools.org>
Subject: With all best wishes
Date: February 14 9:48 PM

Dear Lavinia,

It saddens me that you seem to be taking the changes in staffing as a personal attack. My data simply does not support rehiring you. I'm sure there are other districts looking for a seasoned fifth-grade teacher.

In schools that are thriving, you may find latitude to do as you please. However, your loyalty to the curriculum is not sufficient to maintain your position here, and your level of insubordination is beyond anything I have seen in a professional educator.

I assure you that I care deeply about the education of every child in this school. But this is the 21st century, and the shopworn politics and policies of the 1970s have no place in the modern classroom.

Diana Camelione

From: "Sparks, Lavinia" <sparksl@districtschools.org>
To: "Camelione, Diana" <camelioned@districtschools.org>
Subject: Re: With all due respect
Date: February 14 10:16 PM

Dear Diana,

> "Some rise by sin, and some by virtue fall."
> Measure for Measure, Act II, Scene I

It's this age of inhumanity that will soon be discredited, you'll see. Your attempts to climb the ladder on the backs of our students will come to naught. You too will be tossed aside in the "race to the top." All the specious reforms will be abandoned, and the children will be forsaken once again. No Child Too Small to Fail. Is that what you want your legacy to be?

Mrs. Lavinia Sparks

Section Three
Going the Distance

May

17 / Birthday Bash

Antipathy Brown drew back her arm with
the poise of a hunter flexing her bow.
Her aim was the best in the whole fifth grade,
her power supplied by a trove of woe
too deep and ferocious for us to know.

The tension she felt in her scrawny neck
singed her rosewood cheeks, caused her jaws to snap.
Her five-fingered arrow, shaped like a heart,
rushed to deliver a backhanded slap
that struck its target with a thunder clap.

The one thing worse than an actual birth
was the pomp and nonsense of a birthday.
The attention given the celebrant
caused Antipathy's fragile nerves to fray,
her meandering mind to further stray.

The sprightly singing, the fawning wishes,
the brownies piled high on a flowered plate,
the homemade ice cream, absurdly divine,
were too much for a girl to tolerate.
Her hunger for justice was just too great.

The disdain she held for the privileged child
fed a wrath she mostly reserved for kin,
fueled a fervent desire, an urgent need
to smash the contemptibly fiendish grin
off the face of Felicity Goodwin.

That face, that lovely, intelligent face –
the lips so attractive, the teeth so straight,
the lashes so curly, the features well formed,
the mahogany skin as smooth as slate –
stirred passions impossible to abate.

The force of pure rage caused that face to fall,
its cheeks to burn, its eyes to leak,
its body to crumble beneath its feet
with a gasp, a moan, a shudder, a shriek,
its astonished tongue too startled to speak.

At first the room went eerily quiet.
Then a cheer arose from the anxious crowd.
Antipathy Brown, so crude, so wrong,
so widely admired, justifiably proud,
had all of her classmates hopelessly cowed.

She'd slain the Immortal, Antipathy had.
She'd brought It down at the peak of its prime.
The misdeed was done; the tale was finished.
No one would ask her to pay for her crime.
The feeling of triumph was simply sublime.

What happened next, none could have imagined.
Felicity tumbled the way she'd seen –
part judo, part cop show, part circus clown –
once flash across her expensive widescreen.
She somehow managed a kick to the spleen.

Antipathy screamed. She was dying, she was.
She clutched her side in pain, so sharp she growled,
groaned, collapsed in a heap next to her foe.
When an admirer tried to help, she howled.
When Felicity looked her way, she scowled.

"You witch," she lashed out. "I'll fix you real good."
Well, those weren't exactly her seven words.
In fact, her vocabulary revolved
around six choice insults divided in thirds,
meaning sex, dog, punk, rump, curses, and turds.

Two god-fearing children blurted out "Ooh,"
though most of the kids didn't seem to mind.
They cheerfully swallowed every bad word
till finally Miz Sparks, apparently blind,
accosted the revelers from behind.

"What's going on here?" with scooper in hand.
"Can't I leave you alone for a moment
too see who that was on the phone? My God,
Antipathy, what's wrong? Why are you bent?
Please tell me this brawl was an accident."

"I'll kill her, I will," Felicity swore.
"Die! You hell-bound particle of manure,"
Antipathy hollered. Miz Sparks was through
with these two. They had to go, to be sure.
Such madness had no conceivable cure.

"Call the office," she urged a frightened lad.
"Now, the rest of you children go sit down.
I'm not paid enough to deal with this stuff."
She pictured the beer she would use to drown
another thankless day in Teacher Town.

"The office is busy," Tuan reported.
Miz Sparks would have to find a solution
to calm the combatants, settle the class,
and bring this mess to a resolution.
It was way too late for restitution.

"Princess, take Antipathy to the nurse.
Felicity, call your father to come
and pick you up early. Pedro, go and
get the vice principal." What a bum!
He hides during fights, as a rule of thumb.

I can't take one more minute, thought Miz Sparks.
I'll retire if this administration
doesn't begin to provide assistance,
instead of soundbites and condemnation.
School's gone to hell, and they're on vacation.

Antipathy left, frothing and cursing.
Felicity gathered her birthday cache.
Miz Sparks filed a report in triplicate
about how an innocent birthday bash
turned into a radioactive clash.

The witnesses huddled pretending to
read silently for the rest of the day.
Felicity's friends sought to comfort her,
but Miz Sparks would broker no cheap display
of belated loyalty, try as they may.

Word of the fight was carried abroad by
Princess and Pedro, who stopped every child
they encountered on their way back to class,
dazzled them with details, left them beguiled
by Miz Sparks's fifth graders, so tough, so wild.

When Mr. Goodwin answered his cell phone,
he could barely make out his daughter's voice.
Hadn't he just escaped that crazy school
after cranking ice cream, not his first choice,
and watching some sugar-filled kids rejoice?

What could they possibly want from him now?
He had soldiers to rehabilitate,
stroke victims, children caught in the crossfire,
injured workers he had to teach to communicate
in gestures. Might this emergency wait?

"Put your teacher on the phone," he ordered
his daughter, who was most glad to comply.
"Let the school handle it," he told Miz Sparks,
who grunted, then breathed a protracted sigh,
"I'm afraid we don't see eyeball to eye.

The school could suspend your child for fighting,
which would go on her record, cause a shift
in a heretofore fine reputation,
might damage the esteem and mar the gift
she'd bring the next school, if you get my drift."

Mr. Goodwin listened. He wasn't daft.
Some end-of-the-year reports would be due
at Felicity's brand new private school.
A mistake like this could threaten her coup.
It would all be over in a month or two.

He turned his shiny black sports car around,
an indulgence for his fortieth year
of serving others, his parents, his sibs,
his wife, his daughter. A trade-in was near.
An actual education is dear.

Meanwhile, on a cot in the nurse's office,
Antipathy cried and writhed in torment,
refusing to let Nurse Fine come near her.
The poor girl's angels, usually dormant,
proclaimed what secret her unusual sore meant.

All the world's cruelty, all the world's hatred
had come to dwell in her aching left side,
now bathed in fire, pickled in brine, pricked with
needles of the divine kind, sent to guide
her spirit toward a heavenly tide.

Hearing the dreadful begging and bleating,
Miss Juanita Macabuhay thought for a while
before calling the Browns, her frequent guests.
Their child was verbally violent and vile,
yet they always arrived in clueless style.

Mr. Brown answered, drunk and disordered.
Why couldn't that school just leave him alone?
It was their job to police the children;
his job description: to imbibe while prone.
He was a taxpayer—his business, his own.

"Wake up, Mr. Brown. Your daughter is hurt.
Come out of your stupor, put on your shirt,
bring your medical coupons. I'll summon
a cab to pick up your ass. High alert!"
Brown fell off the couch, his ass to assert.

The vice principal studied his next move.
According to Pedro, the scene demanded
his presence at once. He had to decide
if both prize fighters would be remanded
to their folks' custody, singlehanded.

"I'll be there soon," he informed the boy,
never once looking up from his game of chess,
played against Coach Birdsong every
Friday afternoon. No cry of distress
would keep him from this weekly redress.

He despised Miz Sparks, who acted as if
it was her solemn duty to anoint
him "The Naked Emperor." Of course, the
charge was true but clearly beside the point.
He was merely the Potemkin of the joint.

With schools judged by the public as never
before, fights looked bad. They reset the score
kept by downtown to count how many times
more his school ushered children out the door
than their cross-town rivals. Fights were a bore.

He had better things to do, he recalled,
like recruiting little kids to appear
at the school fundraiser. This year's title:
"Reach the Highest Stars." His mission was clear:
To sell the farm, make the dung disappear.

If tests scores were up and trouble was down,
then enrollment would grow and money would
flow and inspectors would back off and the
press would look elsewhere and everyone could
pat himself on the back. Boy, was he good.

However, while his mind was occupied
with trivial tasks like window dressing,
the Black Queen saw her chance to advance and
capture his Knight while constantly pressing
his King to run. The end was a blessing.

"Is anyone home? I'm here for my kid,"
Mr. Goodwin knocked at the VP's door.
"Can I please have a word, Major Minor?
Sorry to upset these dealings, I'm sure,
But you need to come onto the dance floor.

"My daughter has been an absolute star.
All her years at this school, she's never done
anything remotely related to
what she did today. I've barely begun
to comprehend such a fresh little one.

"Can you give her a break? She's a good kid.
In her heart of hearts, she won't hurt a fly,
Too bad this place has completely transformed
a once-happy kid to one lean and sly.
If you dare suspend her, we won't comply."

"Are you threatening me, Mr. Wise Guy?
I see where your kid gets her outsized nerve.
We've no toleration for kids who fight.
You dare come in here and throw me a curve
By asking pardon she doesn't deserve?"

"Look, the kid's a genius, and we all know
She's here 'cause her mother went to this school.
In those days, this place was a source of pride.
The rules were strict, but the teachers were cool.
Miz Sparks even taught the kids to shoot pool."

Major Minor's left eye started to twitch
At the mere mention of his erstwhile foe.
I must reject, he decided right then,
a pool shark mother using *English throw*.
"I'm afraid your daughter will have to go."

"You're making a very big mistake.
My daughter has newly been accepted
at a private school. But a suspension
on her record might get her ejected.
Your students' safety has been neglected."

Just then, two doors down, a struggle ensued.
A table was tossed, some glass was shattered.
Major Minor barely raised his brow,
The data was really all that mattered.
He watched while Coach and Goodwin scattered.

"Unhand me, you dog," Antipathy wailed.
"I'll have your head on a plate, if you dare
lift my shirt and examine my bruises.
My mother said no one should see me bare.
Kiss my rump, but don't look at my underwear."

The nurse beckoned the men for assistance.
"This girl needs a doctor to check her out.
She's been struck pretty hard, from what I see.
An exam is urgent. Her health is in doubt.
There's one tender spot I'm quite worried about."

The men were reluctant to take a stand.
Women's pain, in general, frightened them.
An injured girl spewing accusations
sometimes found occasion to heighten them.
Sad experience had enlightened them.

As each of them stood frozen and useless,
the sound of a taxi gasping for air
brought a welcome distraction into the room.
While the secretary gathered the fare,
a grumbling giant arose from nowhere.

"What y'all do to my child?" Mr. Brown
pounded his fist on the counter. He was
fit to be tied. Antipathy heard his
voice and leapt from her cot. Relieved, she was,
almost as much as them useless three was.

"Oh, Daddy, you're here. I think I'm dying.
You always say how much you adore me.
If it's true, then please don't ignore my last
request. Be a good dad, for all to see.
I need you to beat someone up for me.

"Her name's Felicity. She thinks she's fine
but she looks like a rhino from behind.
Her braids are fake, her braces stink. She lies
like a dog. Somebody needs to remind
her what happens to kids who act unkind."

Mr. Goodwin's stony countenance cracked.
Who was this who spoke so ill of his spawn?
Could this be the bully that, in her sleep,
his daughter denounced from dusk till dawn?
At a private school, this kind would be gone.

He called Dr. Goodwin, the orthodontist,
who was dealing with a tooth impaction.
He excoriated school dysfunction,
then quickly suggested legal action
as the only way to gain some traction.

"Let's all calm down," Major Minor cautioned.
Mr. Brown spun around, a man possessed.
"What little devil kicked my precious child?"
His hair was smashed, his eyes were wild, obsessed
with exacting revenge, sweet last request.

Goodwin had never been a fighting man,
but now he understood his daughter's stand.
This place lacked control, was poised to implode.
Miss Juanita, the Sane, with phone in hand,
was calling for backup. She was outmanned.

"Ciao ciao." The very greeting caused people to rue
Ms. Camelione, the principal who –
hello and goodbye to you and you, too –
just happened right then to be passing through,
when a mad Mr. Goodwin threatened to sue.

"Did someone say they were going to sue?"
That magic word caused the room to go numb.
The principal, normally divorced from
most proceedings that required aplomb,
was frightened to think what this could become.

Nurse Fine had been trying to catch her eye
to show her the line of students waiting
to register every kind of complaint
about mysterious fumes creating
symptoms that were increasingly grating.

Ms. Camelione again brushed her off,
then looked to Minor for explanation
regarding what had transpired to cause
this unacceptable situation
in which someone mentioned litigation.

Minor adopted the supplicant's stance.
He was used to doing a tortuous dance
whenever his boss called him to account,
which never actually happened by chance.
She flogged him with questions on school finance.

He tried to suggest a change in subject.
A girl was in agony, this was true,
And shouldn't their concern focus on her?
That was the gentlemanly thing to do.
He approached the child to give her her due.

Antipathy coughed and spit on his shoe.
Nurse Fine told Brown to make sure his daughter
saw a doctor post haste. Then, with no time
to waste, she left for another quarter-
time job. Antipathy went for water.

Despite her dying, she somehow found her
way back to her class, determined to strike
Felicity again, and this time do
some real damage, break a tooth or two, spike
a pencil under her skin, steal her bike.

The last bell sounded the end of the day.
Antipathy was soon surrounded by
well-wishers. Felicity jumped on her
bike and sped off, leaving her gifts to lie
on the playground, where all sweet dreams quickly die.

Mr. Goodwin managed to catch his child
less than a mile from home. He hugged her tight
and promised to keep her safe from now on.
Mr. Brown was still threatening to fight
everyone in reach, anyone in sight.

The secretary kicked him to the curb.
Minor turned off his light and locked his door.
The coach skedaddled, as needy throngs rushed
the office, shouting, pushing, vying for
bus tickets, free lunches, and so much more.

Miz Sparks sat at her desk, stunned, defeated.
Her lips were fixed in a permanent frown.
The weekend would only bring new trouble
as the story was told all over town
of the girl who beat up Antipathy Brown.

She shuddered to think what life had become –
an endless series of hopeless dramas
acted by children whose bodies absorbed
the tragedy of communal traumas,
deconstructions, and destruct-o-ramas.

A Japanese beer—that was the tonic.
She hoisted herself aloft, got in gear.
The long walk to the car was arduous.
She went the back way to hide the tear
that marked the sinking of another year.

18 / Culpability

Mrs. Gloria Moore: If you don't mind, I'll begin. The reason we asked for this meeting today is to see if we can come up with a compromise situation. We know we didn't get off to a good start in our relationship, and we're wondering how we can mend some fences. I mean, seeing as how our goal is the same: to give the children the best education possible.

Mrs. Diana Camelione: I'm glad you've come. As I mentioned in my response to your email, the superintendent has asked that you deal with me directly and not go behind my back to his office. He can't be expected to concern himself with the day-to-day running of schools. He has to be concerned with the big picture, the bottom line and the . . .

Mrs. Queenie Johnson: Now that's why we have all these problems in the first place. I'm sorry, I didn't mean to cut you off, but it just seems to me that the management ought to be more concerned with the worker bees, if you follow me.

Mr. Lewis: In all my years as a parent in this District, I have never known the Board of Education to be so unresponsive to the concerns of parents.

Mrs. Camelione: Believe me, I share your concerns. And I consider myself a "worker bee" as well. In my position, I have to follow the policies of the District. I'm sure you understand where I'm coming from.

Mrs. Queenie Johnson: Girl, we are all in the same boat, don't you know? The pressure government workers are under is ridiculous. I told those people at the electric company, if they want Queenie to climb somebody's pole, they better give me more than two weeks of training.

Mr. Lewis: Can we please return to the reason we came here today?

Mrs. Gloria Moore: We're here with a list of demands that I will now read to all the assembled.

> Number One: Stop the Fumes from Hurting the Kids
> Number Two: Stop the Fight from Going to Court
> Number Three: Stop This Fuss from Hurting the School

Number Four: Stop the Firing of Miz Lavinia Sparks, the Best Teacher This School Has Ever Had, May She Live Long and Prosper at Muhammad Ali Elementary School, Which Will Remain for All Time Muhammad Ali Elementary School

Mrs. Queenie Johnson: Amen!

Mrs. Camelione: Is there anything else?

Mr. Lemalu: We have a petition signed by all the fifth-grade parents in Mrs. Sparks's room and then some.

Mrs. Camelione: Unfortunately, I've been instructed to direct any such developments to the District Office of Public Relations. You'll want to mail that to Mr. Cyrus Witherspoon.

Mr. Lemalu: Witherspoon? I went to school with that clown. Is that the best you can do? I wouldn't believe a word that comes out of that dude's mouth.

Mr. Yang: Excuse me, but I thought the superintendent didn't want to concern himself with the day-to-day workings of the schools. So why would a parent petition to the principal be directed to the District Office of Public Relations?

Mr. Hernandez: He's got a point. Don't you even want to know what's in the petition?

Mr. Lewis: With all due respect, Mrs. Camelione, you've got more than just a PR problem on your hands. I mean, you've got kids falling out from some unknown substance, and parents trying to decide whether to pull their kids out of your school. You've got teachers up in arms about the situation with Miz Sparks. You're facing lawsuits from not one but two families that are accusing you of not protecting their children.

Miss White: And you might be facing another one if you don't start protecting my child. You keep kicking out that Brown girl, and she's the only one who keeps the kids from beating up my Pedro. For someone who claims to be a "systems thinker," I haven't seen any action to support that claim.

Mrs. Gloria Moore: Back off, people, you're making Mrs. Camelione cry.

Mrs. Queenie Johnson: Let her cry, girl. If she needs to cry, we got to let her boohoo. Then maybe we can move past our little impasse, you feel me?

Mrs. Camelione: Thank you all for coming. I'm truly moved by your concern for your children. Please leave the petition with me. I'd like to review it before you send it to Mr. Witherspoon. Now if you'll excuse me, I have another meeting to attend.

Mr. Lewis: Whoa, hold up a minute. I think we just got the run around.

Mrs. Camelione: I'm sorry you feel that way. I promise to get back to you as soon as I can about moving your fifth graders out of the back portable. With the weather getting better, it might be possible for them to share space with the cafeteria. I'll check into it.

Mr. Lewis: We'll hold you to that. I mean, it's already May, for crying out loud.

Miss White: I second that emotion.

Mrs. Camelione: I'll do my best. Perhaps I can get you to list your priorities in order of importance. I'm not sure I'll have time to address all your concerns before the school year is over. If I recall correctly, you mentioned three or four things.

Mr. Lewis: We talked about the situation in the portable with the kids getting sick.

Mrs. Camelione: Can we agree, then, to that as the number one priority?

Miss White: The number one priority is protecting the kids from harm, and that includes harm in whatever form it should come.

Mr. Yang: But one situation is a disciplinary matter, and the other is a health matter.

Miss White: They're both about health as far as I'm concerned—mental, physical, social, emotional health.

Mr. Yang: But which is the priority? All these things can't be accomplished in such a short period of time. Personally, I'm most concerned about Elizabeth's physical health. If she doesn't have her health, she can't attend to her studies.

Mrs. Queenie Johnson: That's right, Mr. Ying, health is everything.

Mrs. Camelione: I tend to agree. If the scientific data had been less ambiguous, and if the building weren't so crowded, this issue could have been addressed in the winter. However, if you remember, the complaints weren't so present in the winter when the ground was frozen over. As far as discipline goes, I've been leaving that up to the teachers, and I can see now that I should have stepped in earlier, particularly in Mrs. Sparks's room. Sometimes, when teachers get older, kids think they can get away with the most outrageous behavior, especially when the teacher's back is turned. We need to get a handle on this situation before another child is injured.

Mrs. Gloria Moore: What about Miz Sparks?

Mrs. Camelione: I'm afraid that's a matter that will have to be resolved at the District level. As I'm sure you've heard, there's a union action pending, so I can't say anything more about it. Just rest assured that the utmost care is being taken to preserve everyone's dignity and to recognize the achievements of veteran teachers like Mrs. Sparks, without whom none of us would be here.

Mrs. Queenie Johnson: Can I quote you on that?

Mrs. Camelione: Please do. I'm glad we've been able to come to this understanding. One last question: Has Mrs. Sparks sent you her student narratives, yet? I want to make sure you have time to respond before report cards come out in June.

Miss White: I haven't gotten mine. Have you gotten yours?

Mr. Lewis: No. Not unless William lost it in that backpack of his.

Miss White: I don't know how they find anything in those backpacks.

Mrs. Queenie Johnson: Do you know what I discovered in Princess's backpack? A check from last year's cookie dough drive.

Mrs. Gloria Moore: These kids are a mess.

Mrs. Queenie Johnson: Don't you know it?

Mr. Lewis: Is that all, then?

Mrs. Camelione: Thank you so much for coming. And remember, my door is always open.

19 / Miz Sparks' Student Narratives: With Apologies to the Banished Bard

Sonnet 121   Harry Wilson-Clarke

'Tis better to be vile than vile esteem'd
When not to be receives reproach of being.
Prince Harry, you are so unfairly deem'd
A reckless oaf, misjudged by others' seeing.
They think you lame for tripping over dust,
Find you to blame whenever peace is crushed,
Revile your name the minute stocks go bust,
Suspend their game if protests can't be hushed
By those who think you really aren't so bad.
Why stop a rout because of one poor player?
Last time, our team was saddled with the lad,
Did we complain? No, nary a naysayer.
Besides, a spoiler's not the proper charge.
Your dad's old shoes are simply far too large.

Sonnet 53   Felicity Goodwin

What is your substance, whereof are you made
That millions of strange shadows on you tend?
First Lady of Resolve, you twist and braid
Your classmates' hair to suit the latest trend,
While finding time to lend a helping hand
And share with them your cheese and cracker snacks.
You spare them from instructional quicksand
And offer aid to those whose homework lacks
The proper work to make the favored grades
Or any understanding of the task
Set forth in text more baffling than charades,
Which you derive great pleasure to unmask.
Felicity, your charity untrained
Is adm'rable and easily distained.

Sonnet 60   Renard Balthazar

Like as the waves make towards the pebbled shore,
So do our minutes hasten to their end,
Untouched by you who profits to ignore
When time is of the essence, haste doth end.
Activity, once judged the fate of squares,
Must cease to be the province of the cool,
Whose minds are better spent in unawares
Than Truth, the sweet salvation of the fool.
Why race to be the first to do your work,
When all around you peers are taking flight,
And in the shadows high achievers lurk,
Prepared to answer every question right?
And yet, Renard, as proof of your great power,
I wish you would risk failure for an hour.

Sonnet 12   Xochitl Hernandez

When I do count the clock that tells the time
And see the brave day sunk in hideous night;
I wonder what small good will come of prime,
The factoring and figuring of right.
Then I remember Xochitl's hand held high
And how she read her answer, fierce and strong:
When multiplying two by nineteen by
Eleven gives you four-and-eighteen long,
Then Euclid's Proof and Einstein's mighty schemes
Go hand-in-heart with Aztec double rings,
Reed baskets laced by hands that catch the dreams,
Plus notions of some never-ending strings.
Now kindly will you help me theorize:
Why won't some kids their tables memorize?

Sonnet 139   Will Robinson, Jr.

O call not me to justify the wrong
That thy unkindness lays upon my heart.
For Will is thy name, and thy will is strong.
The best way to stop you is 'fore you start.
The wants of others never cross your mind.
Preoccupied with your intense desires,
A way to appease you is hard to find
When faced with the smoke of your raging fires
Ignited when someone should fail to see
The weight of your needs, your need to have weight,
Or simply decide to plain disagree,
Deny you the chance to participate.
By now your classmates have no appetites
For misplaced priv'lege and mistaken rights.

Sonnet 127   Kiana Moore

In the old age, black was not counted as fair
Or if it were, it bore not beauty's name;
An ugly scent of hatred in the air
Converted easy sentiment to shame.
Kiana, in your skin there lies a power
That paints a knowing smile upon your face
And cloaks you in a bright and lovely bower
To chide the homely bigots with disgrace.
Some wish that they could be entirely black
Not half nor eighth nor quarter as they seem
Apparently, the melanin they lack
Doth bring about a blow to their esteem.
When all around you black equates with woe,
Your stoic pride proclaims it isn't so.

Sonnet 18   Algernon Metoyer

Shall I compare thee to a summer's day?
Thou art more lovely and more temperate;
Rough boys do find themselves in gentle sway
When you insist they be considerate.
They say, "Algernon is the best we know.
He doesn't lie or cheat or make us feel
Impulsive, like we want to pencils throw
Across the room or field trip money steal.
When he is well enough to come to school,
We're soon relaxing at the very thought
Of Al as arbiter of ev'ry rule
Who judges fair all blokes red-handed caught.
If diabetes weren't an epic fight,
Then he would be our everlasting light."

Sonnet 96   Zoe Allen

Some say thy fault is youth and wantonness;
Some say thy grace is youth and gentle sport;
Me thinks thine eyes be filled with loneliness,
The utterly excruciating sort
That comes from having parents who invest
More time in their careers than in their young.
Yet, all the while you strive to do your best.
Alas, your goals and baskets go unsung
By two who matter most and never come
To see you play. The rowdy crowd applauds
Their daughter who can dribble till she's numb
But can't arouse two sleeping jealous gods.
O, Zoe, you are wholly free of blame.
If you were mine, I'd come to ev'ry game.

Sonnet 30   Quincy Smith

When to the sessions of sweet silent thought
I summon up remembrance of things past,
I think about your father, how we fought.
I swore my year with him would be my last.
Yet, here I am some twenty-five years hence,
Surprised to see the same endearing smile
That these long years has dogged me ever since
Your father stuck his foot out in the aisle.
I flew across the room with lightning speed
And landed on a little boy named Sam,
Who luckily was disinclined to bleed,
Since thick he was like old Virginia ham.
Yes, Quincy, your jailed father I did teach.
Compared to him you really are a peach.

Sonnet 69   Princess Johnson

Those parts of thee that the world's eye doth view
Want nothing that the thought of hearts can mend;
Indeed, your charm is tantamount to glue
That sticks to ev'ry patsy you befriend.
Each rumor starts with Princess, this we know:
For drama, you are simply without peer.
The seeds of raw dissension that you sew
Lead always to the conflicts that you steer.
Your unsuspecting comrades think you smart.
Indeed, you are as clever as a snake.
But merely making scuttlebutt an art
Does not of you a politician make.
For that you must bring power to employ
And leave your mark for others to destroy.

Sonnet 27   Jayan Patel

Weary with toil, I haste me to my bed,
The dear repose of limbs with travel tired;
But circling like three buzzards in my head
Are all the questions Jayan thrice inquired.
Three times he asked me why the sky goes grey
Instead of green or purple, brown or tan,
And why do hens not little chickies lay
Instead of eggs that run around the pan?
Three times he tapped me on my shoulder sore
To ask if to the bathroom he could go;
Three times I chose to patently ignore
His pacing like a caged chick to and fro.
Alas, I can't ignore my dreadful plight:
To hear his wee voice morning, noon, and night.

Sonnet 144   Leilani Lemalu

Two loves I have of comfort and despair,
Which like two spirits do suggest me still.
Leilani, of my faults you're most aware,
And blithely point them out to me at will.
The fact that you are, more or less, a wit
Convinces me to grant you have a point.
However, I would thank you not to twit
Me when I'm clearly feeling out of joint.
While levity's a necessary ploy
For getting through an enervating day,
You cannot, when I wheedle you, go coy
As though you don't have anything to say.
We both know how I quite appreciate
The chance to play the devil's advocate.

Sonnet 106   Zachary Jones, III

When in the chronicle of wasted time
I see descriptions of the fairest wights,
I'll note that you began the hero's climb
As squire in the service of a knight.
Whenever he was gone away to war,
Your father bade you guard the castle grounds.
You proved yourself a soldier to the core
The day we found the giant red ant mounds.
While others ran in circles screaming "Fire!"
You grabbed the hose and doused those little beasts,
Then forced the frantic ants into the mire
And covered them with ketchup from our feast.
Dear Zachary, you cause your peers to swoon
And constantly relive that afternoon.

Sonnet 83   Serena Kruse

I never saw that you did painting need
And therefore to your fair no painting set;
For God above is guilty of pure greed,
And to the rest of us must stand in debt.
Serena, how can one as young as you
Possess the kindly wisdom of the years,
Pure graciousness and saintly patience, too,
And courage in the face of earthly fears?
Why do you sit among the clamoring class,
When all your peers are found in iv'ry towers?
Perhaps God sent you here to slowly pass
With plebeius the unforgiving hours
As punishment for lifetimes ever lost.
My God, why levy such a hellish cost?

Sonnet 70   Pedro Brayboy

That thou art blamed shall not be thy defect
For slander's mark was ever yet the fair;
And you, sweet Pedro, Romeo-elect,
Are not to be mistaken for your hair,
Which cascades down your back just like a girl's,
According to the boys who envy thine
Angelic visage and thy sable curls
Both Indian and African entwine.
Let not a mocking cad propose a duel
Lest he might find himself the lesser man
For trying to pin the moniker of fool
On one whose tongue is sharper than his hand.
May they who struggle be the first to say,
It matters not who is or isn't gay.

Sonnet 15   Claire Davis-Walker

When I consider ev'rything that grows
Holds in perfection but a little moment,
And mysteries that only Heaven knows
Seed arguments designed by men to foment
The false divide between phenom and faith
That stirs the heart of ev'ry pious child.
No matter what the learned teacher saith,
The Bible cures what Science has defiled.
I count on you, dear Claire, to make it clear
To minds as bright and fresh as they are thick
That Evolution is Truth premier
And not some kind of God-denying trick.
For we are not so far from chimpanzees.
The difference is a matter of degrees.

Sonnet 120   Kenji Takahashi

That you were once unkind befriends me now,
And for that sorrow which I then did feel
To watch someone past hurt begin a row
With someone else's foot beneath his wheel.
It's hell on earth you can no longer run
Nor leap nor skip nor climb the garden gate,
And all your wishes whittled down to one.
The driver didn't see you till too late.
When people say "It's good you didn't die,"
You wonder how they possibly can know
The pain involved in staying four feet high
When others ever taller start to grow.
I tell you, Kenji, pity brings despair,
And you, dear lad, are brave beyond compare.

Sonnet 37   Jerusalem Tadesse

As the decrepit father takes a delight
To see his active child do deeds of youth,
So I find joy whenever you alight
From bus of shouting children most uncouth.
From whence doth come your unassuming air
With which you conquer hooligans and goons?
Your elders and your youngsters oft compare
Your diplomatic skills to Ban Ki Moon's.
If silence is a virtue, I'm all vice,
And you alone are wise beyond belief.
The point is not to play at being nice
But guard your self-possession like a thief.
Jerusalem, you manage to convey
The kind of grace that words can never say.

Sonnet 19   Marcus Thompson

Devouring Time, blunt thou the lion's paws,
And make the earth devour her own sweet brood;
The world's a torn and tattered ball of straws
With countless millions clamoring for food.
But even with this knowledge close at hand,
Geography still seems the height of joy,
When Marcus leads us over sea and land
With cries of "Landward Ho!" and "Ships Ahoy!"
The Greeks, Egyptians, Persians, Romans bade –
Yea, Tanzanians, Arabs, Lebanese –
Did roam the Silk Routes long in search of trade
With Mongols, Russians, Turks, and Han Chinese.
A fanciful professor with a wand,
You take us to the edges and beyond.

Sonnet 49   Elizabeth Yang

Against that time, whenever that time comes,
When I shall see thee frown on my defects,
I work to guarantee your school day hums
And you go home with minimal regrets.
But on those days your bed becomes your deb,
And 42 is 24 the same,
I worry that your love for school will ebb,
And somehow I will be the one to blame.
If I could see the pictures in your mind
And find a way to make the paper sing,
You wouldn't be in such an awluf bind,
Elizabeth, most words would have a ring.
For music is the heart that makes you beat,
And notes are not dependent on the sheet.

Sonnet 143   Omar Martinez

Lo! as the careful housewife runs to catch
One of her feather'd creatures broke away,
So do I concede I've met my match:
As frisky a lad as exists today!
Why, Omar, where on earth might you wager
Young children free to do as they shall please?
In constant trouble and not one bit the sager,
Quit running away, put my heart at ease.
If others roam in pursuit of faint treasure,
Then failure is all theirs to finally own.
You roam quite freely just in search of leisure,
And treasure you find under ev'ry stone.
If school were taught beneath a giant tree,
Then you a straight *A* student sure would be.

Sonnet 25   Saida Mohammed

Let those who are in favor with their stars
Of public honor and proud titles boast,
While you who suffer poverty and wars
Must bow your heads and mollify your hosts
By keeping your historic knowledge quiet
And drawing no attention to your God,
Lest you should cause great unrest and disquiet
Resulting in the dominoes to prod
Our leaders into serious debate
About the rights of girls to wear their scarves.
Men insecure will seek to regulate
The shining of competing yellow dwarves.
Saida, with your passion for free speech,
Do tell the judge your rights he cannot breach.

Sonnet 6   Elijah Ladu

Then let not winter's ragged hand deface
In thee thy summer, ere thou be distill'd:
Such evil as no child should have to face –
To live to see his neighbors bound and killed.
Elijah, did the prophets speak of hate
Born of the knowledge men as devils ride
And min'ral wars cannot be blamed on Fate
When some things darker in their hearts reside?
Then why do teachers tell their children lies
And act as if the world is made of good?
A boy like you can see it with his eyes:
The world is made of oxygen and wood.
Both Fire and the Forest it devours
Depend upon the Spirits for their Powers.

Sonnet 29   Genevieve Dumlao

When in disgrace with fortune and men's eyes,
I all alone beweep my outcast state,
The lowliest of servants to despise
A teacher left to mourn her sad estate
While others with so little learning thrive
And laugh to hear the joke that she became,
The smartest girl, who once was so alive,
now nothing but a broke and bitter dame,
Me thinks of all the enterprising youth,
Who I have had the fortune to engage
In momentary friendship with the truth
And everlasting longing for the page.
Then cruel Self-Pity bows and takes her leave,
Embarrassed by kind-hearted Genevieve.

Sonnet 140   De'André Jackson

Be wise as thou art cruel, do not press
My tongue-tied patience with too much disdain,
Lest I should lose myself and dare profess
My feelings that you've no cause to complain.
If anyone can deign to take offense,
Then surely, I deserve that special prize,
Though, I must say a word in your defense:
De'André, you move mountains with your lies!
In all my years of teaching ten-year-olds,
I've never had one look me in the eye
And pulverize the fabrication molds
With brazen tales that redden half the sky.
Believe me when I say the sea is wide.
It swallows little boys who test the tide.

Sonnet 84   Netanya Miller-Resnick

Who is it that says most? which can say more
'Than this rich praise, that you alone are you?
Not bothered by what humans did before
Nor worried 'bout the rumblings of a few.
Netanya, you are altogether rare
As Dora Maar or Whistler's lonely mother,
Content to spend long hours in a chair
The subject of translation by another.
So serious and occupied art thou,
The bored will try their best to make you groan.
But all detractors soon you disavow.
They might feel better leaving you alone.
How I admire the way your needles flit!
While others strive to stay awake, my dear, you knit.

Sonnet 91   Tuan Nguyen

Some glory in their birth, some in their skill,
Some in their wealth, some in their bodies' force.
Yet, nothing can surpass the steely will
Of those who have the strength to stay the course.
One such as this—don't let his size deflect –
Inhabits a far corner of the room.
The quick-to-learn must show him due respect
Despite his gen'ral countenance of gloom.
For Tuan exhibits fortitude and grace,
Though in the grip of fear he often lives.
He uses all his patience to outpace
The hares from whom he takes as well as gives.
I'd rather grant the *A* to one who sweats
Than one who takes the test and soon forgets.

Sonnet 2   Isi Edwards

When forty winters shall beseige thy brow
And dig deep trenches in thy beauty's field,
Contentment rare thy aging shall allow –
Self-knowledge quite a pow'rful gift to wield –
The chambers of your heart shall beat serene,
Convinced that you are treasured and adored.
So far as any one of us can glean,
Your silent family speaks of one accord:
Their Isi is the most beloved child
They dared to hope would live beyond a year,
So ev'ry year has been a blessing piled
Atop a mountain high as you are dear.
What you possess no suff'ring can disguise –
Your parents love, the pleasure in their eyes.

Sonnet 35   Bao Pham

No more be grieved at that which thou hast done;
Roses have thorns, and silver fountains mud.
Most students smile when missing only one,
But you fall on your desk. Resounding thud!
Mistakes are how we learn and how we live.
Yet you believe such thoughts in error are.
The smallest failures, you cannot forgive.
When testing comes, your thoughts in terror are,
And no amount of reason makes you feel
An ounce of satisfaction with your gifts.
A pound of trepidation is more real
Than self-congratulations or false lifts.
All contests are unfair unless they're won,
For Bao will always be the firstborn son.

Sonnet III   Cynthina Gregory

O, for my sake do you with Fortune chide,
The guilty goddess of my harmful deeds.
No heart had I to carelessly deride
The off'rings I mistook for harmful weeds.
Small flowers, they were, struggling to be born.
Your face, with'ring in petals of distress –
Humiliation plants a bitter thorn –
I sensed too late the cause of your duress.
Now I have lost you, sweet and tender girl.
No lavish praise will bring you back to me.
What would I give to magic'ly unfurl
A cloak of delicate apology.
Cynthina, I regret you suffer still.
No wonder you of me have had your fill.

Sonnet 126   Efraím Rivera

Oh thou, my lovely boy, who in thy power
Dost hold Time's fickle glass, his sickle, hour;
With ev'ry passing day new wit thou show'st
A poet's touch, a silver tongue thou grow'st;
With gilded words you have a certain knack,
And any inspiration you may lack
Is more than made up by your grace and skill
With which rich repartee our hours fill.
As troubadour you shine by any measure.
The music of your voice is surely pleasure.
Then, what a feckless teacher I must be
To entertain a moment free of thee.
While I adore the way you turn a phrase,
Please Efraím, a trail of silence blaze.

Sonnet 50   Antipathy Brown

How heavy do I journey on my way,
When what I seek, my weary travel's end,
Is subject to defenses and delay
As I must make my aching back to bend
And carry one more soldier from the field
Where she lies wounded, weak and overcome
By misery's unwillingness to yield
And poverty's neglect to make her numb.
Antipathy, your warrior heart cries out
For remedies that won't destroy your soul
Or cause your mind to seriously doubt
That healing hands will ever make you whole.
If Tragedy should someday set you free,
A truly brilliant teacher you shall be.

20 / Sirens

This time, the screaming, they hear,
the hysterical wailing redness
strangles their silent reading,
their heads craning, chests tightening,
hands bracing against evidence of sadness,
one hand making the sign of the cross,
kissing its thumb as a kind of insurance
against memories of the kitchen ablaze,
small children huddled in the stairwell,
father outside with a gun, gesturing,
mother inside with her jaw broken,
signaling, run to the neighbors,
frantically trying to put out the fire
with the dirt from a plant given to her
by her best friend, who urged her not to
marry the import-export man who had bad
things hiding in the overstuffed furniture,
in the false bottoms of ceramic vases.
The sirens bring it all back.
Grandpa lying in the driveway, placed
there by his own nephew, the remaining
twin, up to no good from the time
they were hatched, those boys,
sirens always after them, they can run
like natives fleeing the border patrol,
trying to get home before dark.
Streetlights ablaze till they're not.
Forever night sirens ruining sleep.
When they finally catch her after all

those years of don't tell, someone
finally tells how she uses shoes to lure
poor girls onto street corners that men
drive by and stare. Point blank. Pick one.
Shoes always speak the difference.
If you can't buy an education, you can
always buy good shoes, or someone can buy them
for you. Thigh-high boots. Strapless heals.

2.

She pulls the alarm on a very cold day
and we all line up without our jackets
and wait until the fire engines come
furious around the corner and strongmen
jump down to search for signs of smoke
because this is not a drill and teachers
are scared and huddling as we wait
in the cold and are told not to talk
don't even whisper because we have to
hear what the firemen have to say that
there is no smoke no flame no fire that
someone pulled the alarm who would do that
on such a cold day we all look around for
the eleven kids who are mean enough or
clumsy enough or foolish enough to play
such a prank but three of them are absent
and four of them are standing in line with
the office staff due to having been
in-house suspended when the alarm went off
and the other four are swearing they didn't
do it because they would only do it on a

really hot day when everyone needs a break
not the coldest day of the year when we
can see our breath and hear ourselves
shaking and rattling for once we can't
wait to get inside and feel the heat
of our teachers' voices lulling us
like ceiling fans blowing around hot air
so we never suspect that maybe some kid's
life is on fire and she pulled the alarm
in order to call our attention to that fact,
not, in fact, a sound we wish to dwell upon
because her siren is hurting our ears
it's causing our unprotected ears to
freeze shut, and hell is a cold dull place
where only the deaf can hear the cries
of the living being burned alive.

3.

This time, it's one of your own
in the back of the bus. You feel her
teeth gnashing your flesh, arms strapped
to your sides, eyes clouding your vision,
thoughts roiling your mind, as if she
were your very own child, not this one,
who torments you with unquenchable needs.
Don't know what year it is, who the
president is, can't count backward
from ten. She came to your window,
her sallow hand extended. You stared
a long while before turning away.

4.

Nurses dressed in flowered shirts
shuffle flowers around the room.
You want something sweet. Jerusalem
brings you cotton candy. Cynthina
brings you socks. You're cold. The room
is too small. We can't all fit. Enemies come
and lie at your feet. Some sit on the bed
and tell jokes. Your parents look happy.
Popularity finally shines on them.
This injury is not their fault. The
school should have taken better care
of you. You were in their care, and they
allowed you to be harmed. They sent you
home to die. If the dog hadn't heard you
fall, you would be dead. You describe
Paradise licking your face, tearing around
the basement, barking, whining, whimpering
until she wakes your sleeping daddy. You
seem cheerful, your face not so long
and melancholy. You've even forgiven
Felicity, saying, "She just got lucky.
I could whip her ass anyday."

5.

The nurses whisper. They've seen the
signs before. A social worker comes to
meet with your parents. She asks if she
can interview me. A police officer arrives
with a clipboard. Who did this to you?

It was one of your daddy's drinking
buddies, you tell her. Your mother wails.
I hear sirens. Your father curses. More
sirens. Louder. You cry and scream. Sirens
circle your bed. A doctor tries to take a swab.
You stiffen in protest. A photographer tries to
take a photo. Evidence. All the while, the
sirens keep coming closer. We cover our ears.
Soon they are all we can hear.

by Renard Balthazar

In Miz Sparks's class, we
Don't just write reports.
We demonstrate our learning
By acting out the words.
We test our different topics
And write our different drafts
And practice all the details
To execute the task.
We bring our props and papers
And act them for the class.
We teach each other useful skills
And have some useful laughs.
Our teacher likes to help us.
Our parents help us, too.
And if we need an extra hand,
We ask the likes of you.
So if you doubt our talents
And think our test scores weak,
Then come and let us show you
We know well what we speak.
First, we give the reason
What we plan to teach you
Is something you should know
In case you ever need to.
How to Row a Boat
How to Tie a Tie
How to Tell a Joke
How to Tell a Lie
How to Play the Cello

How to Count the Rings in Trees
How to Sculpt with Blocks of Jello
How to Sing Sweet Harmonies
How to Drive Your Parents Crazy
How to Read an Aztec Calendar
How to Learn While Being Lazy
How to Draw a Manga Character
How to Build a Rocket
How to Twirl a Basketball
How to Pick a Pocket
How to Paint a Waterfall
How to Walk a Tightrope
How to Make Injera
How to Use a Microscope
How to Play Mankala
How to Take Your Pulse
How to Win at Chess
How to Test the Ph of Soil
How to Weave a Colorful Vest
How to Write in Chinese
How to Read and Fold a Map
How to Dance Tinikling
How to Bake a Healthy Snack
How to Train a Naughty Pup
How to Use an Abacus
How to Jump Double Dutch
How to Cook a Goose
First you have to catch the goose
Then you have to kill it.
Then you have to quickly choose,
Fricassee or grill it?

Catch it with a piece of bread.
Grab it while it's napping.
Throw a lasso round its head.
Keep its wings from flapping.
Bring it to the chopping block.
Keep its beak from biting.
Let the pickaxe quickly drop.
Don't prolong the dying.
Pick the feathers one by one
While the blood's still warm.
Soak the corpse in salt water.
Wash your hands real long.
Save the neck bone for the stew.
Take out all the innards,
Stomach, guts and liver, too,
Heart and soul and gizzard.
Bring the knife for butchering.
Chop the bird in half.
Separate the breasts and wings,
Legs and thighs and backs.
Rub the breasts with orange rind.
Coat the backs with pepper.
Plant some cloves, splash some wine.
Brush with honey butter.
Fire the grill with apple wood.
Oil the cast-iron skillet.
Fry some bacon crispy good.
Save the fat for millet.
When the grill is piping hot,
Place the goose upon it.
Put the innards in the pot,

Roast them slow with garlic.
Check the bird from time to time.
Baste with lemon butter, some paprika
and a dash of rosemary and thyme.
Turn one piece, then another.
Smell the juices dripping.
Smell the garlic roasting.
Listen to the sizzling.
Listen to the toasting.
Wash some small potatoes.
Pop them on the grill.
Slice some ripe tomatoes.
Sprinkle them with dill.
Tear and clean some salad greens.
Toss together in a bowl.
Shred some carrots, slice some pears.
Throw some blue cheese in as well.
Mix a little salad dressing,
Honey, oil, and sweet mustard.
Make a lumpy fruit relish,
Cranberries and oranges.
Heat a loaf of fresh French bread.
Fold napkins, set the table.
Do just like the elders said:
Help out where you're able.
Grab the meat thermometer
When the time seems right.
Check the inside temperature.
We want to eat tonight.
Grill the goose till it is tender.
Take it off before it burns.

Now it's time to come to dinner,
Just as soon as Père returns.
I can see him on the road now,
But what's that on top the truck?
In the time we cook the goose, how
He done shot him a buck?
Oh, Maman, we much too tired.
Please don't make us work no mo'.
Mes enfants, y'all be quiet.
Meet your daddy at the do'.
Ask him what he wants to show you.
Ask him what he wants to do.
Then y'all do like he tol' you,
Just the way he tell you to.
Place the meat upon the plate.
Serve it up with bacon gravy.
All you kids can stay up late
Have some pecan pie and sherry.
When y'all a little older,
You can help me with the skinnin'.
But for now, do like I tell you,
Come sit down and eat your dinner.
Now, that goose was sho delicious,
And that bread was genuine.
Them potatoes was pure riches,
And that salad, mighty fine.
I just ate like no tomorrow.
I could hardly help myself.
And my only lasting sorrow
Came when there was nothin' left.
I sure wish I had a little

I could pass around the class,
But I only brought a picture
From my Christmas winter last.
I hope y'all delighted wit'
My simple presentation.
I can recommend you try it
Without any reservation.
You can use this recipe
For anything you snare –
From pheasant to wild turkey,
From salmon to wild hare.
But don't try this on a squirrel,
And don't try it on a possum.
If you must experiment,
I hear principals are awesome.

22 / Damage Control

This is the latest in a breaking news story that resulted from an anonymous tip recorded on the Channel 5 News Line. I'm Josephine Diop with this exclusive.

Southside neighbors are up in arms.
A popular teacher is being threatened with forced retirement.
A principal is fighting to keep her job.
And parents are demanding that their school be rid of what they say is a toxic brew that's keeping their children from learning.

Parents I spoke with earlier today claim the building you see behind me is not safe for their children, some of whom have passed out due to, what the parents say, are toxic fumes.

Kids have even reported mice running down the halls. Parents say they've had enough.

This dilapidated building overlooks a busy intersection in the heart of the city's most diverse neighborhood. It opened to great fanfare some thirty years ago, but parents now say the building is toxic and may be a growing threat to their children's health. The once-shining edifice is now a hulking eyesore covered with graffiti. Mice in the closets, raccoons in the trees, pigeons nesting in the rafters of the gym. Students have taken to calling their school "The Zoo."

Fifth-grade student Saida Mohammed says she once saw a coyote wander onto the playground. "It was over there, near the fence. At first, I thought it was a dog, then I realized it was a coyote, like the one that ate my neighbor's cat. I don't think coyotes should be allowed to come onto school playgrounds."

Her classmate, Quincy Smith, had an experience with a different kind of animal. "One day, we was sitting under that tree over there, and we felt something hitting us on the head, like thump thump, and we saw something up there, and it was throwing down pine cones on our heads. And we started running. And my teacher said it was a raccoon. Yeah, I think it was a raccoon."

Bao Pham agrees. "It was definitely a raccoon. Cats don't get that big."

It might have been that same raccoon, or a different one, who disturbed kindergarteners taking a nap one day. We talked to their distraught teacher, who asked us not to reveal her identity for fear of repercussions.

"It was horrifying, really. The little ones were running around scream-ing. I had never heard anything like it. Maybe it was a fight, or it could have been something more amorous, but whatever it was, it was clearly inappropriate for a kindergarten classroom. I've asked the District to remove the tree, but they haven't returned my calls. I'm afraid it could happen again."

With teachers struggling to keep pests away from their classrooms, it's no wonder the school's test scores are suffering.

One person who agreed to go on record about the problems is Coach Curtis Birdsong.

"Coach, when did you first notice the pigeons?"

"Oh, they've been here for some time. Ever since somebody blew out that window last summer—I think it was some kids with a BB gun who got up on the roof—ever since, we've had pigeons. They've been living in the gym quite comfortably."

"What's the danger of having pigeons in the building?"

"It's really not very sanitary."

"I understand they're fairly messy."

"Well, yes, you could put it that way. You don't want the kids picking up stray feathers or coming into contact with pigeon droppings, which can be toxic to humans."

"Have you complained to the District about this problem?"

"Yes, ma'am. We've complained repeatedly and, frankly, I can't ex-plain the lack of attention. You would think, with all our problems, that we would be at the top of their priority list."

"Have you been able to use the gym?"

"Well, last summer, I went up there and patched things myself, and some parents came in on a Saturday and helped me clean up the place. But after awhile, the pigeons snuck back in. They're fairly resourceful. When I came back after winter break, the place was just a disaster."

"So, what are you doing about PE classes?"

"Well, the weather's been pretty good lately, so we've been able to hold classes outside without too many problems."

"Thank you, Coach."

"No problem."

Perhaps most disturbing of all are reports about students actually passing out due to noxious fumes near the portable classrooms you see in the background. The rather shabby-looking buildings house a fifth-grade classroom, two special ed classes, and a resource room.

I was able to grab a group of students on their way to catch the bus.

"Hi, I'm Josephine Diop with Channel 5. I wonder if you could answer a few questions for me. This won't take long. First of all, will you tell me your names?"

"I'm Efraím. And this is Elizabeth. And I'm Zachary. She's Zoe."

"And who are you?"

"He's Elijah."

"I have to go. I have to meet my sister."

"Well, maybe we can start with you, Elijah. Have you gotten sick at all from the fumes people say are coming out of the ground?"

"No, they just make me sleepy."

"Okay, thank you for stopping. What about the rest of you?"

"I thought I was going to die. I mean, sweat was coming out of my ears, and my eyeballs were getting real big, and I had a headache the size of California."

"Efraím exaggerates."

"What about you, Zoe? Anything you can tell me about the fumes?"

"Some people got dizzy. Yeah, some people got dizzy."

"Has anyone in this group gotten dizzy? Elizabeth?"

"No, but one time, my eyes started stinging, and everybody thought I was crying, but it was because of the fumes."

"So Elizabeth experienced some stinging, maybe like a burning sensation. Were your eyes burning, too, Zachary?"

"Yes, Ma'am."

"Have you experienced any other illnesses or discomfort due to the alleged fumes?"

"They gave me allergies, like a little asthma, maybe. I noticed when I was trying to run a mile, and I got tired. I don't usually get tired. It was the fumes."

"Well, that's pretty disturbing. Asthma can be quite serious."

"Yeah, it was pretty disturbing. They made me sick to my stomach."

"You've been listening to students at Muhammad Ali Elementary School talk about the mysterious fumes emanating from beneath Portable 10. Today, parents and teachers put the ball firmly back in the District's court. Thank you all for stopping to talk. I'm sure our viewers will join me in wishing you a swift end to these problems, which can't be good for your studies."

"Thank you for caring."

"Yeah, thank you for caring. Hi, Mom."

"We'll keep following this story and giving you updates as they come in. This is Josephine Diop for Channel 5."

23 / Miz Sparks Is On Fire and This Ain't No Drill

I waited for Miz Sparks. I hid behind the recycle bin and waited. I didn't hide behind the trash bin because it stinks. I knew she would see me on her way back to the classroom. She had left everybody unattended. Because the principal made her go to the office instead of letting her teach. When she came out, she was breathing fire. I was afraid to get in her way. She was huffing harder than a dragon on Chinese New Year. But then I realized she was crying.

"Don't cry, Miz Sparks."

"Is that you, my sweet Antipathy? Come out of there. It's not sanitary."

"Ooh, something must be wrong. You ain't never called me sweet before."

"That's not true, my little lemon meringue pie. Now what are you doing here?"

"I was waiting for you."

"You see. You're very sweet when you're not being oppositional. Do you remember what your name means?"

"It means I'm smart and highly sensitive."

"Close. It means 'the state of feeling against'. Kind of like I'm feeling right now."

"Did she fire you, Miz Sparks?"

"No. She doesn't have that power. Only God has that power."

"Did He fire you?

"Not yet, strawberry shortcake, not yet."

"Miz Sparks, is it true you ain't coming back?"

"Come here, my little candied yam. What do you think?"

"I think you should stay and fight."

"I've been fighting a long time. Even Muhammad Ali had to retire."

"He's still the Greatest."

"No doubt. He never lost his cool. I wish I could say the same."

"Being cool is overrated. It's better to be red hot mad. If somebody tries to hurt you, you should bite them really hard."

"Is that your best advice, peach cobbler?"

"Yep. You got to leave your mark on the world."

"Come here, honey lamb. Walk with me."

"I ain't supposed to be here. I'm still suspended."

"You don't look suspended. Besides, you've been away from school too long. You've gone back to saying *ain't*."

"I never stopped. I just tried not to say it in front of you."

"So now that I may be leaving, you think you can get away with anything?"

"Who's going to stop me?"

"Oh, so that's what you want, is it? Go on, then. Run ahead of me. Get those legs moving, or I'll catch you, little girl."

I took off like the cyclone in the Wizard of Oz. Miz Sparks was the Wicked Witch without the bicycle. She wasn't green but her broom was on fire, and she was chasing me with it. I ran to the portable.

"Miz Sparks is on fire and this ain't no drill," I banged on the door and shouted.

The kids were inside with Coach Birdsong. They started screaming. Some people got under their desks. I could see them through the window. Zachary and Omar were pulling at the door, so I couldn't get in.

"Let me in, let me in," I yelled.

"Not by the hair of your chinny chin chin," Zachary yelled back.

And then Miz Sparks came up behind me and roared so loud I jumped.

"Open the door," she demanded, "or I'll huff and I'll puff and I'll blow this house down."

I could hear everybody laughing. Coach Birdsong didn't even bother to blow his whistle. He was just shaking his head. Zachary and Omar fell on the floor like the Scarecrow and the Tin Man. Miz Sparks looked at me and whispered, "I'll get you and your little doggie, too."

And that's when I got the idea to bring Paradise to school. If it wasn't for Paradise, I might not be here. The Devil said he would kill me if I screamed, but I couldn't help but scream because he was hurting me.

Paradise bit the Devil in the shin and that's how they caught him weeks later. He still had the mark on him. The detective said I had to testify, so the Devil would stay locked up forever. That's why my dad got sober for true. He said it was his fault for letting the Devil come to his house to play cards.

"Hey, Wicked Witch, is it okay if I bring Toto to school?"

"Sure, Dorothy. Just don't let those flying monkeys catch her."

She flung the door open and all the kids scattered. Then she started chanting in Latin. We had to repeat everything seven times, so Claire would have time to write it all down.

Adversus solem ne loquitor.	Do not speak against the sun.
Alea iacta est.	The die is cast.
Acta est fabula.	It is all over.
Absolvi meam animam.	I have set my mind free.
Excelsior.	Ever upward.
Experientia docet.	Experience teaches.
Illegitimi non carborundum.	Play to win.

She made us shout that last one over and over again.

"Miz Sparks, you done lost your mind," Coach Birdsong shook his head.

"Thank you, Coach Songbird."

"Absum. I'm out of here." And he vanished, just like that.

"Miz Sparks," Marcus called out. "This is a historic day for education."

"How so, Marcus?"

"I mean, first we tried to walk the picket line with our parents, but they wouldn't let us. And we couldn't go to our classroom because of the toxic fumes coming up from the ground—they probably buried some nuclear waste under there—so we had class under a tree, just like the pictures you showed us of the kids in Ghana having class under a baobab tree, except we were under an oak tree. And then you let us start writing our own newspaper. We got to interview people and overhear things we weren't supposed to hear. That's when we got in trouble, and you had to go to the principal's office."

"Go on, Marcus. I'm enjoying your recounting of today's proceedings. I've yet to appreciate their historical significance, but I'm confident you'll get around to that."

"Ooh, Miz Sparks, I know why today is historical. Coach let us play kickball. But Kenji and De' had a fight over whose turn it was to pitch. And Kenji slapped De' upside the head."

"Naw, I hit him first."

"Be quiet, De'."

"Shut up, Princess."

"That was hysterical, not historical."

"Thank you, Marcus. What happened next?"

"We came here to the library. But since the librarian got laid off and they never hired a new one, we couldn't check anything out. We just had to read silently and make sure we remembered where we got the books from. But some of the girls were passing notes, so Coach said they had to read aloud while the rest of us listened with our heads down. Then Elizabeth started crying, so Jerusalem stood right next to her and they read together the poem about the wild swans. It was mysterious and beautiful. But Harry started laughing when they said the word 'lover' and Jayan kept repeating it, so all the boys had to go outside with Coach. And the girls got to play chess."

"We played three games of chess at the same time."

"So what, Isi? We got to learn where babies come from."

"We already know where babies come from. You're the only ones who don't know."

"No more comments from the peanut gallery, please."

"Ooh, Miz Sparks called the girls peanuts."

"We're not peanuts. We're chess nuts."

"Wow. Genevieve told a joke."

"Excellent, Genevieve. Now I'd like to know what the rest of you learned today. Jayan has his hand up. Jayan?"

"We learned that power concedes nothing without a demand."

"Very good, Frederick Douglass. Serena?"

"I am, was, and always will be a catalyst for change."

"Well said, Shirley Chisholm. What else, Elijah."

"We learned to speak truth to power."

"And who taught you that?"

"The American Friends. They helped me and my family."

"Beautiful. May we all learn to be so brave as Elijah. One more. Will?"

"It ain't over till it's over. Yogi Berra."

"Naw, that's Lenny Kravitz, homie. My grandma has the album."

"Lenny got it from Yogi. And I ain't your homie, Zachary."

"You ain't nobody's homie. I was just trying to help you out, dude."

"Don't call me 'dude.'"

"Will, I'm not sure everybody knows who Yogi Berra was. Why don't you tell us."

"He was a famous catcher for the New York Yankees."

"Thank you. Why don't we see if we can finish the newspaper you started this morning?"

"Miz Sparks?"

"Yes, Marcus, what is it?"

"I haven't finished my recap of everything that happened today."

"Well hurry up. Our day is almost done."

"Best of all, you came and found us. And Antipathy came with you."

Everyone turned and looked at me. I was sitting in the back, cleaning out my desk. At first I said, "What are you looking at me for?" But Miz Sparks said, "We're happy to see you."

"Really? I didn't think nobody would miss me. I didn't think nobody would even notice I was gone." My face started getting hot.

"Not notice?" said Kiana. "How could we not notice?"

"Yeah," said Tuan, "You're always causing trouble."

"No, she's not," said Pedro. "Just sometimes."

Everybody laughed. But not me. I started bawling. My skin was all dry and wrinkly because I hadn't cried in a real long time. I forgot how good tears taste. Miz Sparks came over and gave me a big hug and gave me a box of tissue. Then everybody got up and hugged everybody else. Even the boys gave each other boy hugs. Then other people started crying. And Quincy didn't even get mad when Netanya stuck him with her knitting needles.

Then we all got to clean out our desks, even though it was only May.

News from the Fighting Fifth
On the Ropes

Volume I, Issue 1   **Algernon Metoyer, Editor-in-Chief**

DOWN TO THE WIRE
A late breaking report by
Cynthina Gregory

Students were seen playing capture the flag outside the main office. Major Minor came out and said he was going to have us all arrested if we didn't move. Because we were listening in on Miz Sparks who was going off on the principle. You didn't want to witness that. But if you did you know nobody had ever seen such a thing. It was bomblastic like a big explosion. Miz Sparks told the principle to "use your head for more than a hat rack" just like she sometimes tells us to do. You could hear the principle crying. Everybody started running around crazy. Then Coach came by and blew his whisle. We all had to line up and exit the bilding. That's all I know. The real dope.

HERD ON THE STREET *by Bao Pham*
"Wrong and strong." "Got to be more careful." "What the pho!"
DO THE MATH *by Xochitl Hernandez*
.01% fam inc @ \$27,342,212 + 21% kids @ <\$22,050 per fam of 4 ÷ race x gender w/ >9% unemployment ≠ 1 smart country
VERY MAD SCIENCE *by Claire Davis-Walker*
The term "sick building syndrome" (SBS) is used when occupants experience acute health and comfort effects linked to time spent in the building. (EPA website)
SONGS AND SIGNS *by Kenji Takahashi*
Ain't gonna study war no more/Ain't gonna study no more/No more/Ain't gonna study

LETTER FROM A SCHOOLHOUSE JAIL
by Saida Muhammad Ali aka Barbara Jordan
We waited tensely while the grownups decided our fate. Would they let us march? We might get suspended they said. It might ruin our records and then our lives. Only grownups could march. This was our first objection. We were told we had to go to class as usual. This was our second objection. The grownups were worried. They said we might get retaliated against. We didn't care. They wouldn't let us march. Some of us were crying. They said they were going to wear paper bags over their heads so we wouldn't get blamed for our parents. We convinced them to wear scarves instead.

photograph by
Genevieve Dumlao
She hasn't even been
here a year

24 / Renegade Dogs and Other Traitors

I didn't know what to say, what to do.
How I'd come to this passage, I hadn't a clue.
I just couldn't swallow the diluted stew
That passed for education in the red-white-blue.

So I packed up my room with the help of my crew,
Said goodbye to my kids, shed some tears, quite a few,
Then I headed on down to the government cue.
Till I turn 62, unemployment will do.

That TV broadcast caused quite a buzz.
But the principal kept bulldozin' becuz
She didn't want downtown restoring what was
Or claiming "Duty is as duty does."

Several parents decided to boycott the school
Until something was done about the toxic gruel
Masquerading as brain food, post-Brown cruel,
Though seeing their kids on the news—that was cool.

They made signs in private, kept their ideas quiet
To avoid the impression of condoning a riot.
They were open to the idea, might even try it,
If the administration lied again and tried to deny it.

They asked the faculty and staff to try to go native,
Forget the union and their contract, dare to be creative,
"Come on, show all the kids what y'all are made of.
We can't understand who you're so afraid of."

"The principal, she's the one we dread.
When all has been done and all has been said,
We'll have to go way high over her head
To the Superintendent and the Board of Ed.

"But they're the Politburo who sent her here
To foment conflict and engender fear.
She's done a bang-up job; it's really quite clear
She's bound to be promoted this time next year."

I tried to recruit a few friends and fans.
Miss Juanita was in; so was Library Man.
The lunch ladies took a vote, approved of the plans.
"We'll shut down the joint unless they meet our demands.

"We want a much bigger kitchen and healthier food.
How 'bout a better staff room, if you're in the mood?
Could use some calming music. Don't mean to be rude,
But this school has to alter its whole attitude."

If I had fought a little harder, my battle would be won,
But I had papers to correct—they kept coming by the ton.
Thank goodness all the "How To" reports had been done,
Except for the report of a certain someone.

Even though I knew better, I made a decision
To invite Antipathy without the principal's permission,
Once again sidestepping the head of my division,
And making myself a target for derision.

Though I hoped to conceal this bit of deception,
When Antipathy was welcomed with a hero's reception
By the same kids who rejoiced at the time of her ejection,
I had no doubt she could win a Congressional election.

In her hand the child carried a piece of old rope
Tied to a creature needing water and soap.
The kids went crazy, thought the whole thing was "dope,"
While the scrawny visitor looked scared beyond hope.

She barked and she howled and she stiffened her tail.
She stalked and she growled and she started to wail.
She pulled on the rope like she wanted to bail.
She just couldn't stomach the schoolhouse jail.

"This is my new dog, name Paradise.
When she feels like it, she can be real nice.
She's kind of like me, no sugar, all spice.
If you come too close, you'll pay the price.

"I'm going to teach you how to train a pup,
A naughty one who always plays kind of rough.
If you let her run loose, she'll get into your stuff,
And before you can move, she'll tear it all up.

"You might want to know why I gave her this name.
It's only because she was lost when she came.
God kicked her out of the garden, oh, what a shame.
He thought she was way too uncouth to tame.

"He didn't have time for a fallen angel,
So he sent her to find a way out of danger.
He showed her the road that led to a stranger,
Me, Antipathy Brown, who was destined to change her.

"What I didn't know was how she would change me.
She gave me the courage to set myself free
From the devil himself who was trying to claim me.
She taught me to bark up the Knowledge Tree.

"And God came down and delivered me from
An awful fear that was making me numb.
I had lost my voice, he had struck me dumb,
Till this devil was chased to kingdom come.

"Me and my dog, we ran him away.
We cursed him to hell where he'd better stay.
I told the policemen to keep him at bay
Where he can't never hurt nobody no way.

"I didn't think nobody cared about me.
If they did, I thought they'd be able to see
How lost I was, why I was so mean,
'Cause I couldn't tell nobody what I had seen.

"Paradise couldn't tell me what she'd been through,
When I looked in her eyes, I knew she was blue.
She could have been beaten or used for bait, too.
When I reached out my hand, she didn't know what to do.

"I said, 'Come, Paradise,' and I gave her a treat.
I said, 'Come here, doggie, you won't be beat.
Just come have a rest, come take a seat?
Drink some cold water, get out of the heat.'

"And from that day onward, she started to smile,
She went from being crazy to being pretty mild.
So, take my advice if you like my style
And take care of your only begotten child.

"The End. Now, if you want to pet my dog,
And you have enough sense not to try to hog
All her space or get up in her face like a heavy cog
Or scare her by leaping around like a frog.

"Then, you can give her a pat on her side or her back,
But don't handle her rough like she's some kind of sack
'Cause before you know it, she'll be on the attack
And she might even call the rest of her pack."

The students rushed forward with squeals of joy
As if Paradise were some sort of wind-up toy.
They followed the lead of one Pedro Brayboy,
Who urged the lass to bite him, her teeth to employ.

The dog recoiled, and so did her human.
The kids were going crazy, and she was fumin'.
Anti chased Disie around the room an'
Right out the door. Boy, were they zoomin'.

I advised my students to "Go sit down,"
Then I picked up my skirt and went after Miss Brown,
Who looked to be headed straight out of town.
She raced like a fox on the heels of a houn'.

Meanwhile, Coach Birdsong came ambling along.
The Vice had sent him to right a grave wrong –
A renegade student who didn't belong
Was causing a fuss, inciting a throng.

And the teacher, the one who had asked her to come,
Was in strict violation of most rules and then some.
My lavish offenses would cost me a sum,
But until they came due, my word would be mum.

The coach had no intention to nab the teacher.
By all accounts, it would be hard to reach her
As she seemed to be chasing after a creature,
Who was busy ignoring all attempts to beseech her.

Coach managed an ear-splitting, two-fingered whistle
That produced no effect—his thinking was wistful –
So he turned and took off like a heat-seeking missile,
But in no time, his willpower started to fizzle.

"Don't leave me, My Birdie." The voice was Nurse Fine's.
She was fast approaching the coach from behind
As he pursued the girl who would make the headlines:
"School Loses Sight of Student and Speedy Canine"

The police were summoned to join in the fray.
They promised to investigate, come what may.
But no one has learned the fate till this day
Of the wily deserters who fled far away.

Some say we retired to Ecuador
Or got ourselves Shanghaied to Singapore
Or bravely set out to settle the score
By moving our classroom to Bangalore.

But whatever we found and wherever we went
The US of A, we did represent.
We weren't the most learned or the most ignorant.
But we managed to earn all the goodwill we spent.

And when Antipathy Brown was all the way grown,
She didn't have children, she lived all alone.
She started a school for girls in Gabon,
And somehow she managed to send money home.

The End

But Not Necessarily the Truth

Acknowledgments

A public-school teacher saved my life. Her name was Evaline Kruse, and she identified herself as an "American Lebanese." She had a shock of dark hair, a prominent nose, a distinctive voice, and a marvelous laugh. She introduced me to the poetry of Simon and Garfunkel and asked me questions like "Which is faster, a table or a chair?" The letter Mrs. Kruse sent home to my mother, which spoke of my talent as a writer, changed my life forever.

The summer I met Mrs. Kruse, I was eleven and struggling with the overwhelming feelings of a budding adolescent, feelings of which I was deeply ashamed. In her room, it was safe to feel and to think. And if you dared, you could share your musings with the class.

I don't remember much about the other children. The teacher was such a revelation. I was used to nuns who weren't keen on creativity. My mother explained to me that public-school teachers were generally better. So were the books. The classes tended to be more interesting and they typically covered a broader range of subjects. Both she and my father were graduates of the segregated Louisiana public schools of the late 1940s. It was there they encountered the formidable teachers who would brook no excuses. These women and men taught the King's English, for one day integration would come, and their students had to be ready to face the enemy without flinching.

Although they never stopped believing in the public schools, my parents sent us to Catholic schools. By the late 1960s, Los Angeles was already teeming with criminal gangs fighting for dominance of the international drug trade. Public schools had become dangerous places. And the one advantage every private school had over their government brethren was their ability to kick students out at the slightest sign of trouble.

The public schools were required to take all comers. This was their curse as well as their blessing. They would welcome us no matter who we were, not because of who our parents were, or how much loot we contributed to the annual auction.

At the time of my growing up in pre-Proposition 13 California, the public schools were fully funded. I remember walking down the street to Audubon Junior High (where Mrs. Kruse taught) to see a production of *Bye, Bye, Birdie* put on by drama students from Crenshaw High School. I thought they were professional actors. The Audubon Junior High School Orchestra might as well have been the Los Angeles Philharmonic. As far as I was concerned, their playing was masterful. They were only slightly older than I was. Audubon had an open playground all summer. Any neighborhood kid could sign in and check out balls or equipment. The coaches were generous about teaching us new skills. They taught us how to play paddle tennis and ping pong, and we watched future pro basketball players challenge each other in ferocious pickup games.

I had more than my share of brilliant teachers—during my public-school summers, in my Catholic high school, and at the private colleges I attended. For thirty-odd years teaching, I've had the privilege of working alongside some truly magnificent teachers, the great majority of them in the public schools. Their talent, passion, insight, and dedication never fail to astonish me. They seem to survive by their wits alone in these days of diminishing returns.

I wouldn't have thought it possible for the status of public-school teachers to sink any lower than it was when I first started teaching. Now that the government has joined in the attacks, I find it hard to imagine a day when politicians and voters will find the political will to educate all of our country's children democratically. Until our larger ills are addressed—chief among them poverty, income inequality, falling health, and rising unemployment—the public schools will continue to fall behind in international competitions.

Diversifying the curricula, allowing teachers more freedom to be creative in how we choose to meet grade-level standards, reintroducing tried-and-true methods for learning basic skills—all of these changes would help. But nothing would make as much difference as putting more people to work in the schools—a job creation program for nurses, counselors, social workers, secretaries, tutors, gardeners, artists, safety officers, crossing guards, and instructional assistants would alleviate some of the burdens we teachers are ill-equipped to shoulder alone.

It's difficult in any occupation to be ruled by folks who don't have the slightest idea of what they're talking about. For teachers, the current state of affairs is no less than tragic. For students, it's unforgivable. For four decades since the passage of Proposition 13 in California, through the waves of punishing policies that overtook the gains of the civil rights movement, urban and rural children have suffered mightily at the hands of ruinous educational fads and formulas. It's time to let teachers teach again. Until then, all praise to those public-school teachers who face overwhelming challenges every day and strive to meet them with intelligence, grace, and a necessary sense of humor.

Miz Sparks Is On Fire and This Ain't No Drill was brought to fruition with the loving support of Robin Rawles, the vigorous prodding of Nadine Pierre-Louis, the hearty vision of Dan and Amy Peters, the delicious legacy of Jim and Karen Bodeen, the delicate artistry of Sheila Arthur, the supple eye of John Pierce, and the typographical stewardship of Suzanne Harris.

I'm indebted to the Rawles family, especially to educators Ann, Lisa, David, Renee, Robin, Lauren, and Gabrielle, who've joined their talents to a long and proud tradition.

I'm grateful to Eloise Martin, Edree Allen-Agbro, Terry Martin, Jane Gutting, Marcella Keys, Janice Rawls, Karen McFarland, Lois Finzel, Alie Wiegersma-Smaalders, Tina Hoggatt, Tandra Schwamberg, Dee Thierry, Justine Gorman, Alan Miller, Lisa Montgomery, Kathy Lusher, Laura Wall, Constance Hutchinson, Gail Thomas, Niki Riley, Vivian Williams, Kathryn Maria Ritchie, Karlene Wolfe, Carletta Wilson, Savannah Jamerson, Kate Miller, and Kate Smith, who've shared their stories over the years.

To mentors Barbara Earl Thomas, Cheryl Ann Alexander, Alexis Thompson, Anita Morales, Lillie Rainwater, Mende Nazer, Anna Bálint, Martine Pierre-Louis, Mako Nakagawa, Joyce Dennison, Jane Sarmiento-Schwab, Michael Schwab, Linda Brown, Mary Lee Colby, Kelly Allen, Mary Ellen O'Connell, Maureen Sweeney, Kathleen Alcalá, Karen Toler, Teri Lewis, Christine O'Connor, Tim Noonan, Marjorie Lamarre, Cathy Sims, Glenda Smith, Maureen O'Neill, Sam

Green, Eric Johnson, Leslie Sager, Georgia McDade, Laurie Kazanjian, Judith Roche, Diane Studley, Erie Jones, Libby Sinclair, Julie Trout, DeeAn Nakagawa, Linda Walsh Jenkins, Sally Nemeth, Angie Nall, LeeAnn Stivers, Victoria Bernstein, Christopher Drape, Julie Savas, Agnes Seong, Jenny Pohlman, Carla Arellano, and Beth Brunton, I couldn't have laughed my way through this ill-conceived writing assignment without you.

To all my students—you know who you are—I hope this finds you well.

As for Carmen Ufret-Vicente, Leah Opiniano Bui, Laurie Rostad, Mo Fain, Tom Sunderland, Connie So, Cheryl dos Remedios, all my partners in crime and fellow rabble-rousers, hats off for your steely dedication and willingness to make posters.

Finally, if not for the prayers and faith of Laurence Pierre-Louis, neither my teaching nor my writing efforts would have borne much fruit. To her memory, and to the memories of Manfred Rawles, Venise Jones-Poole, Cary McCrae, Elise Powell, Rosalie Monica Spooner-Jordan, Mabel Darensbourg, Theodore Darensbourg, C. Bernard Jackson, and Evaline Khayat Kruse, I offer this little paean to passionate educators everywhere who won't let go of the bone.